HOLYLAND

A novel by

Richard Curtis Hauschild

First published by Dog Ear Publishing
4010 W. 86th Street, Ste H
Indianapolis, IN 46268
www.dogearpublishing.net

ISBN: 978-145750-249-1

This book is a work of fiction. Places, events, and situations in this book
are purely fictional and any resemblance to actual persons, living or dead,
is coincidental.

This book is printed on acid-free paper.

Printed in the United States of America

SPECIAL THANKS TO
JOHN and ALICIA McCAREINS
Who have believed in me and supported
my writing from the beginning

CHAPTER ONE

SONIA

Writers write. Being the adopted daughter of a literary family certainly did open doors for me, but my part of the bargain has always been to keep creating interesting works. In this part of my contract, this journal, I no doubt will fail because I am a poet and really don't know how to make long sentences of prose work to any good advantage. What you are reading are more like organized notes and snippets from scraps of paper I have collected daily since I left home a few years ago after graduating from high school in Fond du Lac, Wisconsin. That town is the middle of my story and this writing represents the rest of it so far (I am now 23 years old). The beginning, as most early youth, is hard to remember other than I know I was born in the Sudan, was adopted, and spent my first years in Boston. My mother is Molly Costello, the author, journalist, and biographer of my grandfather, Roland Heinz, who my sister Melanie and I called Papa. If you recognize his name you know he won the Pulitzer Prize twice (!). I know that was a tough act to follow for my Mom's fiction. Maybe that is why I became a poet; I sought my own sunlight. Anyway, before this becomes too boring, I will tell you that today I am sitting in the Air France VIP waiting room at Charles DeGaulle Airport outside of Paris waiting to meet up with my sister, Melanie, who as a doctor, will no doubt notice that I have a bullet wound across my right cheek. Someone almost killed me, Sonia Fara Costello: 'The Poet-Laureate of Darfur.'

I was asleep on this soft Parisian morning in August and lost in one of those states that travelers attain after they stop moving for a while. I was asleep and yet I knew I was dreaming. My dreams often confuse me and this particular one I wanted to remember. It was a sepia tone seascape and I was aware that there was some danger in the water. I kept trying to walk inland, but the sand was deep and my progress was too slow. I knew that something was coming out of the water behind me that I didn't want to see. I felt mild panic…and then a hand shaking my shoulder. Thankfully, it was Melanie.

"Hey, sis, wake up," she whispered in my ear. "It's me."

I know I was smiling even before I opened my eyes because I was being rescued. Seeing Mel always made me smile anyway. She is so beautiful. Melanie was adopted out of Viet Nam and we grew up knowing we looked different, but that was all. We were sisters in every way. After completing her medical school and internship at the university in Madison, she had joined *Caduceus International*, traveling the world to hot spots that needed free doctors. She and I laughed that she was the practical healer and I was the spiritual counterpart. We never planned it that way when we were growing up. It just happened. There may have been some competition at one time on who was going to save the world first, but reality whacked that idea. It always does.

"You were talking in your sleep again, Sony."

"In what language?" I asked. I spoke a little of everything these days.

"You said 'go away' in English and your face was frowning. Bad dream?"

"Yeah, traveler's dream."

"Oh yeah, they are the worst."

Melanie paused and I could tell her eyes had locked on my bandage.

"What happened?"

There were a couple of ways I could have gone with this, but Mel has truth serum eyes so I told her the real story. I think it was in the press already anyway.

"I got shot at. It creased my cheek."

Mel wanted the story, but her instincts went to the wound first. "Can I have a look?"

"Sure," I said and turned my head to make it easy for Mel to peel back the bandage. I watched her eyes and saw her wince.

2

"Ouch. That was close, Sony. Where did this happen?"

For some reason I was a little embarrassed and I wondered why. Could it be because I was smiling like a goof and it sort of hurt?

"I was in Nairobi," I said. "We went out to a place in one of the slums to see a performance. A band with dancers. We kept it low key as far as an entourage and it was really neat until…"

"Until you got shot," said Melanie.

I knew she was going to finish that sentence because it had happened before.

"I don't think they were aiming at me, but yeah, I got shot. It was so weird. I mean I heard the shot and looked that way and I actually saw smoke from a gun, a rifle I think and then…well…"

"What?" asked Mel.

"I swear it was like I saw the bullet coming. I moved my head just in time or…you know."

My sister stared at me with those Asian eyes. Some people stupidly call them inscrutable, but I read my sister's eyes pretty well after all these years. I saw surprise, fear, and then a smile began there at the corners.

"Close only counts in horseshoes, eh?" She spoke with a very bad fake Wisconsin accent. She had never picked up the real one like I had.

"It was close, I got lucky, hey?"

"You got lucky again," said Mel. "How many lives do you think you have, Sony?"

She was referring to my brushes with danger since I left home to become an NGO worker. At least that's where it all started. I should fill you in. Mom says to always assume the reader has no idea who you are. That would not have been hard to do a few years ago, but somehow fate stepped in and made my face famous. I am not bragging about this fact; I wish it were not true. You see, I became the subject of an international incident only a few weeks after I arrived in Darfur. I was only 20 years old at the time and no one knew me from Eve. It all changed in a heartbeat. I became the international darling of the press when I went missing from a camp. I became their Cinderella when I came out of the kidnapping alive. My face was everywhere for a while and that kind of fame led to the popularity of my poetry. I would not recommend this road to literary success, but it worked for me. Armed Sudanese bandits turned me into a genius. Irony is so ironic.

I smiled at Melanie and unconsciously fingered my Claddagh necklace. It was a gift from Des O'Connor, someone Mel didn't like. She took notice.

"What do you hear from him?" she asked, her eyes focused on the golden hands holding a heart. "You see him lately?"

"Not for a few months…and don't look at me like that."

"Sony, he's a married man who only wants what he can't get. And he's way too old for you. If he's giving you lucky charms it's a freaking joke."

"Let's drop it." I knew all too well what Des wanted. He had already gotten most of it.

"Okay by me," she said dismissively.

So, reader, you got the name of Desmond O'Connor out of me early. Mel is right; he is a piece of work. More on him later. There have really only been two men in my life, or should I say my heart. One was the son of a Mexican migrant worker that I knew in high school and the other is an Irish poet who makes me dizzy. They both dance around inside my head like orphaned electrons. The quick change of subject allowed me to deflect the light of inquisition on Mel.

"How's Ray, sis? You see him lately."

This was a bit of a snip as Melanie and her husband Ray Hitowski Jr. spent most of their marriage at opposite ends of the earth. Ray was a lawyer based in Los Angeles; Mel had no base. They have been very much in love since first sight, but their careers have conflicted badly. But, then Mel's eyes always lit up when she thought of Ray and now was not an exception.

"I saw him last at Harry Stompe's funeral, but I think I may be seeing more of him soon."

Quick note: Harry Stompe was an old family friend and associate of Roland's who also happened to be my mother's and my publisher. Harry was much more than that to all of us. His passing in June brought us all together to say goodbye to one of Papa Roland's oldest friends. I felt a great era had ended with Harry's death; an era born in the days of hand-written manuscripts and gone in the age of word processing and prolific, but vacant pop writers. I loved Harry, but I was talking to Melanie so my reverie was timed out by the blink of an eye locked on my sister.

I caught the innuendo and the huge smile and took a wild guess. "You're quitting CI? Moving to L.A.?"

"Yes and no."

"What does that mean?"

"Well...," Mel said and then gave what I realized quickly was a very pregnant pause. "It means you're going to be an aunt."

My eyes went instinctively from her face to her stomach where the miracle was taking place. This news meant more to me than I could have anticipated. I will remember this moment forever because it seemed our family was doomed to never expand. Mom was in a relationship, but it had begun late in her life and, though I think she wanted a child, there would be none. I was meeting men, but not the marrying kind as Mel would often remind me. I never seemed to slow down enough anyway to consider having a family. And Melanie was, as I said, so career-minded (along with her husband) that this news seemed like much more of a miracle than it actually was. And yet, miracles should not be rated in that way; any-how.

"When?" was all I could say.

"Well, I am due early in January. What is that, a Capri-corn, right?"

I nodded thinking why is my sister, the scientist, consid-ering the Zodiac sign of her baby? It didn't make sense, but I loved that for some reason. "Where are you going to have the baby, sis? Los Angeles?"

"Well, actually, I think I want to have it at Ghost Farm."

"What? Not in a hospital?"

"No, not in a hospital and I want Mom to be in on the whole thing. You think she would like that?"

"Wow, Mom would love that. But, what about Ray?"

"We'd all be home, Sony. Christmas in Wisconsin and then…" She pointed at her tummy.

I had almost forgotten that Ray Jr. was originally from Wisconsin, too. His father was the famous rock star, Crazy Ray and his mother, Carrie Stirling Gabler was a long-time friend from back there, too. Crazy Ray had died several years ago after he and Carrie got divorced and she later married the famous celebrity photographer, Mike Gabler. Carrie's mom, Pat Stouffer is my mom's best friend. Having the baby in Fond du Lac would be perfect for everyone.

Before our flights were called, my sister and I caught up on each other's news. She was on her way to L.A. and I was going back to Wisconsin for a short visit with Mom and Owen. I needed to decompress from Nairobi. I sat and listened to Melanie's phone call to Mom and smiled as she delivered the baby news. When she told Mom that she was going to have the baby in Wisconsin, I read Mom's reaction through Mel's expression. Suddenly, I couldn't wait for Christmas. I got handed the phone and quickly confirmed that I would be in Milwaukee in about 24 hours. Owen was going to pick me up and I looked forward to that very much.

Owen Palmer is a veterinarian who, besides living with my mom, has his practice in our old yellow barn at Ghost Farm. I love Owen like the father that I never knew. He is my hero. He is a poet in his own way; deeper than most men. God help me, but Owen and Desmond O'Conner look kind of like they could be brothers. So weird.

CHAPTER TWO

BIM

Okay, here I am on this blistering hot August day sitting in my garage in Fond du Lac, Wisconsin. You say, so what's new, Bim Stouffer? Well, what is new is that my lawn chair is now a wheelchair. I don't need the chair all the time, but it is useful. I can and do use a walker, but it's tricky. My face looks like I got a fish hook pulling away at the left corner of my mouth. My left arm is mostly useless, curled up and resting in my lap most of the time and I don't talk too good anymore. Yeah, I had a stroke about eleven months ago. Shit happens. I got in the habit of writing notes to my wife, Pat with my good right hand because I was embarrassed about my slight slur. Now this small saving grace with the old Sharpie has turned into a sort of hobby. I write all day long about everything that happens in my world, which isn't much, but it kills the time.

Funny thing about the stroke is I don't remember too much about it. I guess I was sitting in the garage one day having a morning beer and the next thing I knew I was in the hospital and my life was changed all around. It took me a while to realize what had happened and then it all sunk in. The fact that certain things would never work again was depressing as well as scary. So what do you do? I went home an invalid complete with the chair, the meds, and some day nurse who taught Pat how to maneuver me. I let the doctors and therapists push me around for a while until I got the lay of the new land. Then I told Pat I wanted to go back to the garage. I thought she would be exasperated, but she just smiled. She was even going to have a ramp built from the back door to the driveway, but I said no. I couldn't give in that much.

So what has changed since all this happened? The simple answer is not much. I still get a beer or two every day. I still watch the world go by down the driveway. The view sure as hell hasn't been altered for cry-eye. But, now it seems I am some sort of manic journalist as though all the words in my brain have spilled down into my good right hand and seek the notebook like crows on a bag of French fries. Roland would love it. In fact Roland inspires me daily to keep going. He must have felt this compulsion, too, when he wrote those long and complicated books of his. Of course, I can't write like him, but writing like me is okay. Besides, the writing, I discovered that if I could regain my old crustiness, folks wouldn't feel sorry for me. I began to write letters to the local paper about what I saw, heard, hated, and loved about this town. The editor, whose name is Jack Reinholt, asked if I would do a weekly column and I liked the idea. *Bim's Garage* was born. I liked the notoriety (they don't pay much), but I wish people would stop honking when they drive by the house.

"Hey Bim, what are you writing today?"

It was my wife Pat. Somehow she had snuck up on me, which I guess is not too hard to do these days.

"Oh, you know, Patsy, I just noodle along. I write about nothing and that news editor thinks its pure genius. Got 'em all fooled, for cry-eye."

"Why don't you let me get you a laptop, Honey? I don't know anyone who actually writes in longhand anymore. Even Roland Heinz wrote on a computer."

It was not the first time this had come up. "Hah, you keep forgetting I'm mostly a one armed bandit these days."

"So you peck away with your good hand. It would still be way faster…and neater than what you're doing."

"Maybe, but I don't trust those damned machines. Besides, why would I want to do anything faster? Do you know how hard it is to slow down Time these days? I want it slow and steady. Besides…" I wanted to change the subject. "Besides, Roland had a lot more to say and less time to say it than I do. And ain't it time for my beer?"

Pat smiled at me. She and I had both gotten lucky. We had married mostly because we were both lonely neighbors and the marriage could have gone either way since we had tied the knot drunk in Las Vegas. But, this crazy love some-how worked and I will never question the complexity of the human heart. We just landed in a soft place together.

A car horn blared loudly from the street and Pat's head jerked instinctively toward the sound. I just stared at my wife in admiration. My legs wanted to leap up out of the chair and propel me to hug and kiss her. They couldn't quite do it spon-taneously, but my mind did the deed. That is how writing works—you let your mind do the hugging and kissing.

Those are the preliminary sketches of my new life, but of course, there is much more going on just below the surface of Bim Stouffer. My old friend, Roland Heinz often mentioned the Dark Ages of Life in his books. Those periods, or cycles when bad things begin to happen merely because it is their time. In *The Tap Root he* wrote about how at certain times even the birds disappear. Well, I think I am in trouble because here in Fond du Lac you never go too long without seeing or hearing a cardinal. They are even the mascot of the high school teams. I ain't heard a red bird in a while and now even my wife is a little too quiet. She is keeping something from me because she doesn't want to add to my own troubles. Don't people get it that if you love them you spare them nothing with silence and denial? For instance, I know how my wife dresses when she is going to see her doctor. She had the doctor dress on when she said she was going to the store about two weeks ago. Then she went again two days ago. Same dress. Two hours later she comes home with only a small white bag, the same bag my meds come in from the pharmacy. So I don't ask any questions because I know she will tell me when she is ready. The dress. The birds. Dark Ages. Jesus Christ, Roland, help me. Okay, I found it. Page 381:

Garnet was riding her pink three wheel bike on a day like no other. Weather could be a soothing cool cloth sometimes after the dog days. In the back of her head she knew she looked ridiculous and passing cars would remind her with a cruel toot. It didn't matter today. She would sleep well now that the window fan could be turned off, eliminating the white noise that distorted her recent dreams. She felt the muscles buried deep in her heavy thighs begin to warm with the exertion and it was a powerful sensation. She was gliding to the big lake.

At the park on the south shore of Winnebago the horizon lengthened and the full tapestry of the sky was a dizzying blend of mares' tails and dark profile clouds, ripe for interpretation. She found her favorite bench and laid a plastic bag of cookies next to her. She ate the cookies one by one, but the usual comfort they gave her was not forthcoming. Something was wrong. There were no birds. No gulls, no robins, not even a crow.

She now remembered her dream of the night before. She had stood on the parapet of a stone castle alone watching an army of men marching toward her. There were hundreds of armed and faceless warriors coming to lay siege. Somehow she knew they could not breach the walls of her castle, but neither could she ever leave it. And thus began the Dark Ages of her dreams. She sensed no escape would come to her in sleep for a long time.

Garnet shivered at that remembrance and then began to cry. She pushed the cookies away and stared at the army of dark clouds that marched across Winnebago to The Ledge. She felt she could not be more alone or more betrayed by her creator. The summer with its heat and cloying humidity had ended, but now the day like no other had become sinister. She shivered and thousands of soft arm hairs were raised on bumps of subtle terror. Then from nowhere one bold crow, the only bird on earth, hopped up on the bench and snatched a cookie. It paused only long enough to make eye contact with her and then flew away with its prize.

Garnet drove her three wheel bike back home as fast as she could. Home was her castle of stone and she needed to be inside the walls. It was only later, after the day like no other had faded to a starless black that she began to realize that the crow had been sent to cheer her. Always look for the messenger bird. Always.

Roland Heinz's books are a comfort to me, but damn it where is the messenger bird today? Just then my cell phone chirped. At least it was kind of like an electronic bird call. Jack Reinholt was on the line wondering if someone could come by and pick up my column because it was deadline day.

"Why don't you get a computer, Blm? You could email the article in and save a lot of running around."

"My wife made the same observation."

"You got wi-fi over there?"

"What the hell is that? We still got a hi-fi, I think."

"Listen," said Jack, "I think we have an old laptop lying around here somewhere. I'm going to send it over with the courier. He will set you up and answer any questions on how to use it. Okay?"

"Waste of time."

"Humor me."

"Tell him to bring a six pack."

"Hey, I can get anyone to write a column like yours."

"Go ahead, Jack."

I relished the long moment of silence on the other end of the phone. We both knew that his readers loved my bullshit.

"Give it a try you old goat. I gotta go."

"Pabst Blue Ribbon, Jack."

"Fuck you."

I love the newspaper business.

CHAPTER THREE

MOLLY

It has been an unusually hot summer so far here in Pipe. Owen and I talked about perhaps installing central air conditioning for the house, but we decided that would be the wrong thing to do. Surely there were heat waves in the past when the old farmers lived here, although I cannot imagine milking cows or making cheese in this kind of weather. But, more than out of consideration for the old farmers, we thought that Roland would be offended by the modernization of Ghost Farm. He still haunts the place now. It's his call.

If you think I am being cute talking about ghosts at Ghost Farm, I am not. We have come to accept as a fact that the restless spirit of Roland Heinz (and somehow his famous character, Garnet Granger, too) are fluttering about; whispering at night and placing odd things in odd places. If this sounds a little 'out there' well, maybe it is unless you live here. Owen and I have rather enjoyed our haunting. After all, the ghost of Roland Heinz not only nudged us together as partners, he keeps us together as lovers and kindred spirits of our own. In short, Owen Palmer and Molly Costello sleep in a hot and humid upstairs bedroom in a one hundred year old farm house because we do not want to offend the dead with the addition of an air conditioning unit. Makes sense, right?

There is a thick layer of ground fog this morning and I can't see a thing out of the kitchen window. I am up and making coffee while Owen takes a shower directly above me. I have to be careful what I do in the sink as it affects the water temperature up there. If I wanted to hear him yelp I would turn either the hot or cold tap on full blast and wait for the expletive, but then I love that man too much to ruin his shower. I love him more than anything. I should explain what we have going between us. Actually, writing it down helps me to define what it is. I know it is wonderful, but there was a difficult beginning for us. The middle part is great and the future looks much brighter than the view from the kitchen window right now.

Owen has his veterinary practice in our old yellow barn. He used to have a clinic over in Long Lake and the beginning of the end of that era came on the day I met him when I brought in our sick barn owl. On that fateful day, the owl died, Owen was attacked by a cougar (of all things!) and we fell in love. Looking back, the last part was not all that simple, but we managed to hang on to that mystical 'something' just long enough for it to catch fire. Now with his office in the barn, our driveway and yard are busy places where there was once mostly silence. I found that it was the noise of his clients' comings and goings that allowed me to relax my writer's block and crank out three more novels. One of which titled Kettle *Moraine*, is being made into a film in the area this summer. It has the whole region buzzing. I did not write the script for the film, but the director, Jon Greenwood calls me to consult on details all the time.

I suppose this is to be expected since *Kettle Moraine* is the thinly disguised story of Owen and my love affair. It was a best selling novel a couple years ago and my most profitable work so far. It was the first time that I wrote about something so close to me and set in the place where I live. I had no idea it would be popular, but then Roland gained his fame when he stopped writing about a faraway war and focused on peace in Wisconsin. Anyway, Owen and I secretly love all the attention. Neither of us are embarrassed that all the neighbors know (or think they know) about how we fell in love. Besides, film rights money for the book paid for the new x-ray and anesthesia machine in the clinic.

The ground fog was just beginning to clear when Owen came down stairs and slipped his hands around my waist. He smelled of Irish Spring soap.

"I'm off to the airport, Mol. You sure you can't come?"

"Oh, how I wish I could. I can't wait to see Sony, but I promised Pat I would go with her to the doctor today."

"Yeah, I know. Any idea what's going on with that?"

"She said it was nothing to be worried about."

"Which means she's worried?"

I turned away from the sink and faced Owen. It was always like looking into the sun for me. He dazzles. I nodded an emphatic yes to his question.

"Honey, you go get Sony and I'll take care of Pat. That's today's assignment. Maybe it'll turn out to be nothing." Of course, I didn't believe my own words. After Bim's stroke I thought the Stouffer's had enough trouble, but I knew certain health issues were remorseless in the land of cigarettes, alcohol, and deep fried food. In other words I feared the dreaded 'C" word.

After Owen left for Mitchell Field in Milwaukee, I got dressed and headed over to Pat's to pick her up. I could not help feeling somewhat giddy after talking to Melanie yesterday. The job of telling the Stouffer's was left to me, I guess. Pat is Melanie's husband's grandmother, but maybe Ray didn't know about the baby yet. I had decided to tell them in person just to see their faces. Having a grandchild or great grandchild was such good news and Pat would be delighted. Bim, too. But, how could I be so happy if my best friend was sick? I was still conflicted when I got to their house and headed up the driveway. I no longer tried to bypass The Garage Sitter. He was waiting for me.

"Good morning, Miss Perfect."

"Good morning, Bimster. When are you going to stop calling me that?"

"When you become Mrs. Perfect."

"Don't hold your breath."

Bim gestured for me to sit in his old folding lawn chair, but I hesitated.

"Sit. She's still in the bathroom," he said and the tone was insistent so I sat down next to him, facing out down the driveway. I have been here many times over the past few years.

Bim and I have gotten even closer since his stroke turned him into a scribe. We share something more than an occasional beer now.

"You know why she is going to the doctor, Mol?"

"Do you know? What can you tell me?"

"I know just enough to know something is not right. Lord knows I study her enough to know things like that."

"Like what, Bim?"

"Like the way she hides pain and worry behind her smile. She is sighing a lot lately, too. Not a good sign for someone who never sighs. And most revealing is that she is spending more time out here in the garage with me. And it ain't just my stroke neither. I get around pretty good on my own now."

All of this is not what I wanted to hear. I had learned to trust Bim's instincts.

"Well, I guess we'll find out soon enough."

I heard the screen door slam shut and turned to see Pat wearing that painted smile. I saw it and immediately thought that Bim was right. Something was wrong. There was no cigarette in the middle of her smile. She sighed when she saw me and then composed herself quickly. She walked over to us waving a copy of the morning paper.

"It says they're going to be filming downtown this morning. Isn't that exciting?"

"I know," I said while studying my best friend's body language.

"That gal that they got playing you, Molly don't look nothing like you," Bim offered.

"Yeah, she's way prettier," I said.

"That's total bullshit," said Pat.

"She ain't so hot, Mol, "said Bim, "but the guy playing Owen is prettier than all of us. Anyways, they're closing down Main Street for the entire morning. Some of the merchants are grumbling, I hear."

"I hear they're all getting paid a lot more than they would on a normal morning. People just like to bitch," said Pat. She was looking at her watch.

"We should get going, huh?" I said.

There was a lull in the morning just then. It seemed like the birds all got quiet and there was no street noise. The leaves on the trees did not move and the clouds froze in the blue sky. Pat looked at us like she was about to leave on a long trip. She sighed again.

"I know you two are worried about me, okay?" she began. "I'm scared, too, but I think we should go find out what's up before we hold the wake here in the goddamned garage."

That statement seemed to give her face a look of courage.

"Oh Patsy…," Bim muttered.

"Oh shit, Bim, don't start the oh Patsys. Whatever this is I'm coming back home here later and making dinner just like I always do. We'll have a long talk then when I find out the lay of the land, okay?

She went over to him and gave him a peck on the head, but Bim took her hand in his good right hand and held on. He was the actor now, smiling just like some director in his head told him to. "What we having for dinner, Honey?"

"Old Fashioneds and tuna salad sandwiches."

"Do I get an Old Fashioned?"

"You do tonight. Molly, you wanna stay for dinner?"

"I can't. Sony's coming home later, but I'll take a rain check. I love tuna."

Then I remembered my big news. I decided everyone could use some good news. "Melanie's pregnant!" I blurted out. "We're going to be grandparents, you guys! You two are going to be great grandparents!"

"Jesus Christ," said Bim. How'd they do that being so far apart?"

Pat was happy-shocked. "Oh my God, how wonderful!" She turned to Bim. "They must have closed the gap some-where along the line, eh?"

Pat kissed Bim again and we headed off to the Agnesian Clinic with the two most opposite of emotions on earth riding along in my back seat.

CHAPTER FOUR

DESMOND

My little flat, more specifically the place where I write, is a mess. It reflects my life, I suppose. At least that is what my wife told me before she tossed my sorry ass out of our house in Dublin where she remains so she can be closer to the friends upon whose shoulders she cries daily. Well, of course, I put those tears in her eyes and set her friends against me so who am I to send angry darts off in her direction? The marriage was doomed before it began because she fell in love with a poet and I fell in love with idea of being married to an adoring fan. Now it is I who love a poet with little chance of winning her. I might keep trying if I can emerge from this self-pity.

And so begins my semi-bachelorhood here in Limerick because it is close to Shannon Airport, one of my many forms of escape. Technically, I am still married as no papers are or ever will be forged. We will simply be apart. As you have noticed I cannot even write her name because even though it once was so beautiful to my ear, it now stings me there with bitterness.

There once was a poet named Des
He lived all alone in a mess
He's a poet of fame
But, can't write her name
Tho, the tabloids will save you a guess

And that will be my one and only Limerick from Limerick. God in Heaven, I want to delete it right now, but let it stand. I deserve even my own derision for how I treated her and what

I put her through in the public eye. And therein lies the tale I have decided to tell—even if only to myself.

In the best of times, when Limerick was my weekend retreat, I sat in this room and wrote brilliantly. I had purchased a little bookstore a few years ago with a flat above it and now it is my permanent home, I suppose. Poetry flows from me here, but so does despair. I am romantic, clever, and as Irish as the dew on the peat. I am also published in seventeen languages that all lose something in translation, but one: Gaelic. But, then bloody English lends itself to the words so while I tend to think in Erse, my late publisher, Harry Stompe, insisted I submit in English because most of my work ends up in little bookstores in America. They tell me I sell well in a place called Wisconsin and I don't doubt it considering my association with that state's little darling. Well, everyone loves a scandalous romance, it seems. Even those distant folks squeezing at the teat of a black and white cow in some smelly barn. At least that was my vision before I got to know the girl and where she came from. I woke up this morning with the notion that I needed to do something about it all. I could call it a research trip for my work, but, if I am honest, I would admit that I want to go to the source of her and learn some things I don't know yet about her. Besides, escape is my *modus opperandi*.

I decided to run my mad plan past my friend and associate, Cedric Young, who runs my book store, which by the way, is named Blackthorn Books. Cedric is a black man from South Africa, who is very bright, handsome, and quite gay. I found him doing my books in the back room of the store with the kettle on as usual.

"Oh, Boss, I'm glad you popped in," Cedric said. His spectacled eyes only glanced once above the ledger to identify me and then he finished some scribbling.

"Trouble, Ced?"

"No, not too much anyway. But, why do you keep writing checks in pubs on the bookstore account? Use your damned credit cards, man."

"Sorry, sometimes I am a bit addled by the time I need more cash."

"Pardon me for saying so, but you seem addled most of the time lately, Des."

"That's how poets are. We feed off the agitation, digest it, and crap out verse."

"How poetic."

Now Cedric may be a poof, but he owns the mind of an astute observer and compulsive problem solver. He is also sly and sarcastic, traits I admire, but not necessarily when aimed at me. Understanding all of this I feed him my personal data as one would feed a computer. His take on things are obtusely dead on. I paced waiting for him to assess me. I could hear his brain humming. Why was he taking longer than normal?

"Will you stop pacing, Des. I think I know how to fix you, if such a thing is indeed possible."

I spun on my heel and took a chair across from his desk, piled high with my problems big and small. "Yes?"

Cedric put his hands behind his head and smiled his perfect white smile as he delivered his wisdom. "Go away."

"And where should I go?"

"Oh, you already know that part."

"I do?"

"Desmond O'Conner, you come in here with a faraway look and I know that you want to follow that look to the far-away. So I think who or what is faraway? But, then it doesn't take a genius to know who, but before I book you a flight I need to know where."

I was busted, as they say.

I went over to the bookshelf and pulled out an atlas of the world. The fact was I wasn't quite sure the place name of my destination. I felt Cedric's eyes boring a hole in me as I fumbled through the pages.

"Aha, I have it. In the USA, north of Chicago. Milwaukee. Can you get me a flight to Milwaukee, Wisconsin?"

Cedric was already typing information into his computer. "When do you want to go?"

"Today."

There was another minute or two of keyboard work.

"If you want to leave today and I assume you are after that girl…"

He paused long enough for me to confirm with a nod.

"If you leave today I can get you to Wisconsin, but you would have to arrive at Green Bay. Austin Straubel Airport."

"Is that close to…Pipe?" All I really knew about Sonia's hometown was its unusual name.

"It's about the same distance as Milwaukee. You'll want a car rental, too, I assume?"

"Yes, nothing fancy."

A few minutes later Cedric handed me a printed itinerary and boarding pass. "You leave Shannon tonight at 6:10. You'll chase the sun to Chicago and then change planes and arrive in Green Bay, Wisconsin USA late tomorrow afternoon. Should I book you a room?"

"I'll wing it," I said.

"Oh, really? You arrive in a strange, foreign city, step off the plane, and…wing it?"

"That's what I do best, Ced." I was smiling, but he wasn't. He seemed to switch from helpful aide to scornful accountant in the briefest of instants.

"Desmond, would you like a little dose of truth for a going away gift? You, my friend, are running out of money rather quickly. Since the death of dear Harry Stompe, you have no proactive publisher. Your books don't sell much anywhere anymore. Your wife is still using your credit cards, although I should add, with less reckless abandon than you do."

Cedric paused to catch his breath. "Anything else?" I inquired.

"As a matter of fact, yes. You haven't written anything new in months. You hang out in the pubs and rely on your reputation to have your back slapped by sots who have never read a line of your poetry. In short, you are about to fail. And all because you have an itch for that young American that you can't scratch. What do you think is going to happen in Wisconsin USA? You don't even know if Sonia is going to be there, do you? My god, man, think about some of this on your long flight to nowhere."

It is pretty hard to shame Desmond O'Conner, but Cedric had done a fine job of it. I wafted my hand at him and went upstairs to pack. His words did however stick in my head and yes, I did think about my life all the way across the Atlantic Ocean. I was truly winging it. I had tried calling Sonia Costello several times recently, but only got her voice mail which I would never speak to. I thought it was enough to have her see my missed call. Besides, I had nothing to say…on the phone, that is.

My theory, though flawed, was to travel to the center of her universe and whether she was there or not, to learn something about her. In the back of my mind I knew that this thinking was produced mostly by my restless nature and my financial ability to do whatever I wanted to do. Learning I was running out of money only spurred me on to do it before I could not. You see, I was instantly attracted to Sonia Costello and then not longer after, crossed over into that other room in the heart, love. It is a laughable, sophomoric notion until it happens to you. I guess I fell in love with her picture on the cover of every newspaper and magazine in the western world. Lots of people did that. But, when I met her in person she turned me to smoke with her eyes. I have been in a state of smoke every since. Smoke blows in the wind; it rises and it falls. It changes shape as it undulated to where? Heaven? Smoke is my metaphor. Sonia Costello is my heart's nebulizer.

CHAPTER FIVE

SONIA

I should explain my celebrity since being a poet almost never makes you famous. My goal had always been to somehow go back to the Sudan and first, find my people and then help them. Okay, idealistic, but the drive was so strong when I was a girl and it was possible to achieve. Despite the urgings of my family and high school counselors I joined a non-governmental organization called *African Answers*. It sounded perfect for me. I would be trained in language, customs, food distribution, and some medical applications. The training was in Florida and then I would travel with a group to Darfur.

I was adopted in the Darfur region of Sudan, but beyond that fact, I knew nothing of my birth or family. With the help of my mother's investigative skills I knew I had been rescued from the aftermath of a militia raid on a village. My parents were presumed to be dead and I was given to a Christian mission group and eventually offered for adoption to Americans. That is were my mom found me; on a web page full of black faces. She said that my face jumped off the page at her and she began the process of making me her daughter. I know it was more complicated than that, but that part of my life never really mattered to me.

I am writing this on my flight back to the USA and I did that thing where you look out the window and see your own reflection superimposed against the sky in the window. I confused me for a moment and then somehow I thought again about Ali Assan.

"You are not one of them, Miss Sonia."

Those were the first words I heard when the long scarf that had been tightly wound around my head was removed. I was suddenly aware of a flickering fire and then smell of hostile men. I felt the burn of rope on my wrists and the darkest fear. I had been abducted from the *African Answers* compound near a refugee camp in Darfur. My kidnapping had not been part of a raid, but rather, I later learned, a selective theft for a possible ransom bounty. In the back of my mind I feared rape and death, but I kept shoving those thoughts away. It worked at first, but then I would remember hearing how these bandits sang songs as they raped. I blinked and focused on the source of the voice. He was much taller than the other men around me. He spoke pretty good English with maybe an Arabic accent.

"You are not one of them," he repeated and I latched onto that phrase.

"What do you mean? Who are you?"

"You work for those people, but you are not one of them. You have Arab blood, Miss Sonia and that makes you one of us. You are too beautiful to be a slave. The men of your blood have rescued you. You are safe now in the arms of your people."

I was dumbstruck. I remember how the first waves of reality came over me and how the final reserves of fear and panic that I had been holding back came surging forward in my brain. My first clear thought was that I wanted my mother. I think I had heard about that reaction before and it made me cry as though my emotions would help me to escape or at least awaken from the nightmare I had entered.

"Don't weep, Miss Sonia. Perhaps you will go home very soon. You can go back to writing your pretty poems about this ugly land. You can go back to your West Constin."

I quickly realized that this man knew where I was from, but had very little understanding of it. He tried to sound soothing and charming, but now I believed him to be ignorant and that scared me even more. At least he had sent the others away leaving us alone.

"Who are you?" I asked trying to control my sobbing.

The man stood up and he seemed even taller than I thought. I could see he was wearing American sneakers under his long dishdasha. He was bearded with a large hawk nose and his skin was light brown like mine. In fact, he did look more like me than the people I was in Darfur to help. I knew I had some Arab blood, but until that day I didn't know it was any big deal. I watched him pace as though collecting his thoughts. We were in a sort of army tent and I could see that it was light outside. I saw nothing else, but I heard men's voices very close by and, from time to time, there was a ruffle in the canvas as someone pushed upon it. I recognize that as a threatening gesture.

"I am called Ali Assan. And I am very pleased to meet you, Miss Sonia, though I understand that you are not at all pleased to meet me. But, you should know right now that I am the only person standing between you and the savagery of fifty men who would take you on the ground and make you wish for death. Do you understand?"

I nodded. I was really scared now. He was no longer speaking of my safety.

"You came to the Sudan with grand ambitions, yes? You would care for the poor people and write poems, yes? You would go home and feel like you did some wonderful thing for your people, but as I said; those are not your people. Your people are waiting outside this tent for you to be given to them to sate their lust and anger at your betrayal of them. Only Ali Assan keeps them away."

Then he disappeared. In fact I have no recollection of anyone coming into that tent for what I guessed was three, four days or maybe longer. I was left alone, tethered to a pole with only a little water and a crude chamber pot within reach. I do remember being fed something. I think I was drugged. For those blurred days, all I could do was listen to the singing of 'my people' who taunted me day and night. I eventually surrendered to sleep, which for me was like giving in to death. I fell into a death-like abyss of hopelessness where my dreams became an afterlife.

I awoke with a start at the sound of a loud thump beneath me. It took me a good two seconds to realize I was still on my

Air France jet and the sound was the landing gear getting ready to kiss the runway at JFK. Anyway, that is how I remember Darfur, my abduction, and Ali Assan—like a dream that comes and goes. Sleep is the medium for those memories now. Nightmares and rapid heartbeats. Despair and hope. Most of the experience is captured in my collection entitled *The Lost Circus*. That collection of poems and CNN made me famous, along with countless reporters, bloggers, and the photographers who made my face as famous as the other kidnapped women, who happened to be pretty. My face and story sold my poems. A wildfire had started in Darfur where there was nothing left to burn.

On my flight from New York to Milwaukee, I found Ali waiting for me once more in the depths of my travel fatigue. His memory, like my capture, is always going to be lying just below the surface of my life. It was a horrible ordeal, but my salvation was incredible. I suppose I owe both of them to that man and because of that he is one of the strongest male presences in my life so far: the taker and giver of my future. I never hated him because I believe he was inserted into my life for a purpose. The ordeal made me stronger and made me a better writer. Having said this I never wanted to see him again.

I woke up on what I guessed must have been days later, but could have been weeks in the tent to bright sunlight in my eyes. The door flap had been flung open to reveal a low sun backlighting a figure I recognized as Ali Assan. I knew something was going to happen. I was totally scared, but also excited. As my eyes adjusted he just stood there. Gusts of wind rocked the tent and then I became aware that the wind was the only sound. There was no one else outside the tent. The landscape opened all the way to the bright sun disc on the horizon.

"Good morning, Miss Sonia." He turned and looked behind him. "As you can see we are alone."

"What's happening?"

"Ah, freedom is happening today."

I was still rattled from the days of continuous threats and fear, but I did notice that my heart began to speed up. "Freedom?"

Ali entered the tent and the flap blew shut behind him. The bright light was gone, but when my eyes readjusted I could now see his face clearly. He was smiling.

"Yes, you are free now. You will be going home. Isn't that the news you have dreamed about?" He then cut my tether to the center pole of the tent. I tried to stand, but my legs were too wobbly.

"Don't try to do too much too soon, Miss Sonia. You need some food. I have brought you some sandwiches and Gatorade." He opened a bag he had slung over his shoulder and did produce food and drink. I never knew you could smell a sandwich, but then I had never been this hungry.

"Gatorade."

"Yes, and cheese sandwiches. It is all I could get for you right now."

Ali Assan pulled up a stool and sat down. Again I noticed the western athletic shoes and blue jeans; socks that had the Nike swoosh.

"You have many questions. I will try to answer them, but we must leave here as soon as you feel strong enough to travel."

"Where are you taking me?" I asked. I still had some idea that this was some sort of cruel game. Scenes from bad movies flashed through my brain. They always set you up and then take you down again.

"I am driving you to the border…to Chad. You will be met by a diplomat and he will arrange to fly you to Rome where someone from your organization will take you back to the USA."

"How long have I been here? Why did you kidnap me?"

"Yes, you sit there and eat and I will explain. You were taken…"

"Kidnapped!" I blurted out. The point seemed important just then.

"You were taken by men who used to be Jangaweed. Since the new government has been in place they are now merely called bandits. Bandits steal things and they stole you. They stole you for money. Kidnapping, as you call it, is part of the economy in this horrible place. You have been here for seven days. You looked surprised. You have been drugged a little. Sorry for that. You have also been given cans of liquid food to survive. Anyway, they had been waiting for you, Miss Sonia."

"Waiting for me? What does that mean?"

"It seems your story preceded you to the relief camp. People talk. It was common knowledge that the granddaughter of famous American writer was coming to Darfur. It was also known that this American girl had a wealthy mother, who was also a well known writer. Books mean nothing to these people, but they understand that 'famous' means rich in the West. When you came to the camp and the infiltrators saw how beautiful you were, the interest level grew. The bandits wanted to steal you and get a ransom, but they also wanted well, they wanted you very much. You know what I am talking about?"

"Yeah, I got that part. And you protected me? How did you manage that?"

Ali stood up and paced a bit. He was thinking this part out. I think he knew that every word he said would be in the press in few days.

"Yes, I saved you. Let us just say I have a power over these bad men."

"Money?"

"Money and fear."

"You aren't one of them."

"So smart, Miss Sonia. Neither one of us is the person people think we are."

I got the rest of the story, at least as much as he would allow me to hear, on the way to the Chad border. The first paparazzi showed up in Rome, of course. I had no idea how the world had been captivated by my captivation. The whole thing had gone viral in the various media. Okay, I know it was my famous family and my face. I have been told I am pretty. Looks fuel stories like these. Plain girls don't make the news. Plain girls don't get taken away. Plain girls don't become famous in a week. I sometimes wish I was plain. I sometimes lie.

The bottom line is I never knew who paid my ransom. I assumed at first it was my mom. She had been contacted, but was still franticly trying to gather money and deal with the FBI when she heard I was released. My NGO didn't have money for ransoms. Harry Stompe, my publisher was working with my mom. It was a total mystery and Ali Assan would not solve it for me.

No one ever came forward. It maddens me sometimes that he or she won't allow me a conclusion to the story. It dangles out there just beyond the flashing light at the tip of this jet's wing in the blue ether. It just flashes away.

CHAPTER FIVE

MOLLY

Waiting rooms at hospital and clinics are designed to be bright and pleasant. They are supplied with diversions like TVs with cable news reminding you that the rest of the world is in distress, too. Magazines, I noticed, are flipped rather than read, but they absorb some of the time. While I waited for Pat I slipped into people watching. Adults pretended to be unconcerned and little kids were wonderfully oblivious. There was a lot of agitated body language that screamed for relief and I watched as various patients returned to the outside world to meet the concerned. It was the smiles, both fake and real that I watched for. Good news and bad news produce different smiles, different gestures. I thought I could decipher them until Pat emerged after a full hour of consultation. I only knew that she was seeing Dr. Lu, Roland's onetime oncologist. Pat was not smiling at all…until she saw my frown. Then the waiting room exploded with the light of information.

"Non-Hodgkin's lymphoma. Treatable," she whispered in my ear and then she kissed me on the cheek.

On the way back to her house I got the whole story. A large lump had developed under her left armpit. It had grown at an alarming rate and while it was not painful, it was annoying and she could not keep from touching it, which made it a little sore. She had been biopsied twice, which is what she was keeping from me and Bim. She said she wanted the whole story before worrying anyone. I listened with relief, but I still felt concern.

"So what do they do now?" I asked.

"Well, they are going to remove the tumor. Then I get chemo and radiation treatments to make sure the area around the node is cancer-free. From there we just have to wait and see if they killed it. Fun, huh?"

"I wouldn't use that word, but what you are telling me is there are usually good results with…what you have?"

"Dr. Lu says statistics are on my side. Of course, I have watched too many Packer games where statistics are on their side and they still lose. What I am celebrating is the fact that I do not have an aggressive cancer that is going to kill me before I see my great grandchild. Not too mention the fact that Bim needs me more than ever."

"I need you, too, Pat." The quick glance that we shared at that instant was the best of our friendship. It was real human emotion spoken by the eyes. I noticed her eyes were sparkling and beautiful. I knew then she was going to beat it. I also knew she was the closest friend I had ever had. Our newest bond was made of pure gold.

I left Pat off to deal with Bim on her own. I saw him sitting in the garage in his wheelchair and watched as Pat walked up to him and pulled up a chair. As I backed out of the driveway I read the anticipation in his eyes. I drove away knowing he was about to be relieved of most of his fears. He was going to be dealing with some bad days ahead, but Bim is surprisingly tough. I think he got some of it from reading Roland's books. Roland and Garnet knew the ways out of hell. I had used their atlas often myself.

I was about to get melancholy when my cell phone rang and I saw it was Owen. I had assigned him the ringtone of 'Camptown Races' and I answered it before the doo-dahs.

"Hi Honey, what's up?"

"Sony's plane is late so I am calling up chicks to pass the time."

"Funny."

"You don't sound funny," Owen said.

I knew I didn't. I was still thinking about Pat.

"Sorry, dear, I just left Pat and Bim."

"What's the verdict?"

"Well, the good news is she has a treatable type of cancer. The bad news is she has some tough treatments ahead."

"How's her attitude?"

"Actually, pretty good. She seemed relieved, but I don't quite know how to read her"

"Listen, Molly, I deal with animals who don't talk. You learn to trust their moods and reactions…their eyes. I can get a pretty good idea even from a cat how it is doing."

"So?"

"So, listen to your friend. And keep an eye on her, too. If she says she is okay, then you have to be okay. And her eyes won't lie to you or Bim. Get it?"

"I think so."

"Good because I can hear something in your voice and it sounds unsettled. I know how you project. You are very good at borrowing trouble. Finding doom and gloom where there is hope."

I was silent for a moment. Owen read me like a book…even over the phone.

"Molly?"

"I'm here. I was just thinking about how much I love you. When do you expect Sony to get in there?"

"It looks like she is on approach right now so figure we'll be home In a couple hours. What's for supper?"

"We're grilling. I have some brats and cold salads."

"She'll love that."

At that moment I heard the beep of another incoming call. It was Jon Greenwood, the film director. "Jon is calling, honey. Call me when you guys get close. Okay, bye."

I switched calls. "Hi, Jon, what's up?"

"Hello, Molly. How are you?"

"Okay…" I was projecting again. I sensed something was up.

"Hey, I am almost at the end of your driveway. You mind if I stop by for a sec?"

I had just pulled in myself and I looked behind me. A van was turning in. "Sure, I see you. Come on up."

When the van came to a stop I could see Jon was not alone. There was a woman with him and I immediately recognized her. Who on earth wouldn't? It was Sarah Dylan and she was the actress who was playing me. Suddenly, I was very nervous. I felt invaded by the 'other me.' The prettier, more talented and successful one. Of course, Sarah didn't look like me at all either, which helped me to realize that all of this film stuff was just play-acting. And yet, it was all such a wonderful diversion. That's what movies are.

"Molly, I would like you to meet Sarah. Sarah this is Molly Costello." Jon was beaming as he watched us confront each other. More theatrics.

I was trying to clear my throat as we shook hands. Sarah felt warmer than the day. She looked at me over the top of her sunglasses and then her smile exploded on me.

"Molly, oh my god, I have read all your books! Even before I got the script. I'm a huge fan. In awe really."

I was caught off guard, but well, I'm Irish. One good dose of blarney deserves another. "And I have seen all of your films." It wasn't a lie, but in the theater she was bigger than life. Here in my yard she was real life-like and her beauty was subtle yet dazzling. I immediately wanted to keep her there to show her off to Owen and Sonia. My mind raced ahead, but I was trying to 'act' cool.

"I wanted you two to meet," said the nearly forgotten director. "Actually, Sarah insisted, didn't you?"

Sarah nodded without taking her eyes off me. Maybe I was being studied.

"Well, let's go inside," I said. "Get out of the sun at least."

I don't know how we ended up at my kitchen table instead of the living room, but that was as far as we got. A few minutes later that setting seemed natural. I offered them iced tea, but Jon asked for a beer so we all ended up with a bottle of Leinenkugel Summer Shandy and soon that sad, anxious morning was swallowed by a lively afternoon.

"Tell me about your...Owen," Sarah asked kind of out of the blue. I knew that this meeting had been set up so she could study me, maybe get some ideas about playing me; but I was caught a little off guard regarding Owen.

"What do you want to know?" I replied.

Jon jumped in. "What's the first thing that pops into your head when you think of Owen?"

I took a deep breath while I thought this out, which was not what they wanted. "When I think of Owen, I think of me. He is like a character from one of my books that sprang from my head when I needed to write about a hero and a lover. I wrote him before I met him and then spent my life looking for the real man to fill the part. In that way, I knew he was that guy the moment I met him. Then like a movie romance, it took some time and plot twists to finally get us together."

"Interesting," murmured Sarah Dylan. "Do I get to meet him, too?"

"Actually, he and my daughter should be home anytime now."

"You mean Sonia Costello is going to be here, too?"

Sarah looked hopefully at Jon, but he shook his head. "We have to go, Sarah. We are shooting a night exterior this evening over in New Prospect and well, both of us have to be there for it to work."

New Prospect by night. I could not help but think about Junior Bondurant, a guy who almost came between me and Owen. He was mercifully renamed in my novel, but I knew who he was. In reality, I had not seen or thought about him since I wrote the book a few years ago. I didn't pursue it with Jon.

"Okay," I said, "call me when you both have a night off and we'll have dinner and you can meet my partner." I had always hated the word partner and at that moment it really sounded like the word itself was watering down our love. Something happened to me in that instant that would change my way of thinking, but I would not define it until later. Jon and Sarah left about twenty minutes before Owen and Sony arrived. I spent that time on the phone with Pat giving her the Hollywood dish. She ate it all up and for that time we never even alluded to her illness. She is a strong Wisconsin woman: wife, friend, homemaker, and a realist who enjoys the unreal.

CHAPTER SIX

SONIA

I spotted Owen near the baggage carousel. He didn't see me so I could kind of sneak up on him. This man seems to have an aura around him that everyone notices. I think perhaps it is the scars from the cougar attack years ago. People see a handsome man with facial scars and whatever story or explanation comes to mind results in a smile. Owen is special and I want him to be my father. There I said it. I hugged him around the waist from behind.

"Guess who?" I whispered.

"I know that sneaky hug," he said as he turned and faced me. I looked into his face and smiled like everyone else.

"Oh, Owen, I missed you."

"I missed you, too…" His voice trailed off as he saw my bandage. He whispered to me so no one else could hear. "Your mom and I already heard about your near miss. You okay?"

"Yeah, fine. Word travels fast, huh?"

"At the speed of light these days. It was a rumor and then in the news even before Melanie called."

My bag came around the carousel just then. I pointed and he grabbed it.

"Let's talk in the car," he said and we headed for the parking garage. He and I both noticed some people staring at me with that 'is it you?' smile.

When we finally got onto the 894 Bypass Owen very subtly began his questioning. I knew he was prepping me for what I was going to tell Mom about the crease on my cheek. He was giving me a chance to sort it all out, which I admit I had not done before. I had learned from my kidnapping how to bury unpleasant thoughts deep inside. Now just being in Wisconsin was making me feel safe enough to talk, but I was choosing my words carefully.

"Sony, you still there?" Owen asked. It was his second question after the one about what happened.

"Yeah, I'm here. I'm back. I'm safe. What do you want to know?"

"I asked you what happened in Kenya."

Traffic was light, the day was bright, I'm a poet right? "Someone fired a gun and it almost hit me in the head." It was a start.

Owen's head was nodding, taking in information and wanting more.

"Do you know who shot at you or why?'

The rest just came out like a dam of denial bursting. "I don't know who shot me, but I saw someone there that I recognized."

"You did? Who? Your life is maybe just a little too exciting for us."

"I know," I whispered and the tears came. They were bound to come. I was releasing every secret to Owen. "God, I never wanted this. I never wanted the fame or anything. I wanted to help my people and then I found out they weren't my people. I wanted to be a poet and then I realized that my poetry was giving away too much of my soul to strangers. To their interpretation. I thought it was neat the first time I signed a book and the first time I saw my picture on the cover of a magazine. Now what, I'm a target? Owen this sucks so much. I just want to go home."

I know I sounded like a little kid, but I could be a kid with Owen and he knew it. He was as gentle with me as he was with his clients.

"Okay, take it easy, honey. You are almost home. Look, every car has a Wisconsin plate. There are black and white cows up ahead. Mom is at Ghost Farm and God is in Kloten."

I smiled immediately. Kloten, for God's sake. We drove in silence for a few miles and passed out of Milwaukee into the northwest suburbs and then the countryside. I was working up the nerve to tell him the rest of the story. I knew he was waiting for me very patiently. When I saw the first Holstein I felt safe enough to continue.

"Okay, here it is. I think I saw Ali Assan in the crowd in Nairobi. I had thought I had seen him or someone who looked very close to him and he was staring at me when the bullet buzzed. I didn't even know I was nicked, but he did. He was watching me, too. I saw him turn and look for the shooter before I put my hand to my cheek and saw blood."

"And you're sure it was that guy?"

"No, not courtroom sure, but I have thought it over and it is too much of a coincidence that someone who looked like him was there at that moment."

"But he was not the shooter?"

"Absolutely not. I never saw the face of the shooter, but I think I saw the gun. I mean, you know, I saw a flash from behind where the dancers were. It was like I followed the bullet and moved my head. I think it would have killed me if I didn't move."

"Sony, I have to ask this, who would want to assassinate you?"

There it was: the word 'assassinate.' The word reserved for the planned killing of famous people. How could that word and I ever have been linked? The word made my stomach churn. It made me not want to be me anymore. One word. I could not answer Owen's question so I just sat there mute.

"Okay, I'm sorry I asked," he said. We can change the subject, but it is going to come up again when your mom gets you alone. You should know there have been some calls from the FBI already at home. Them and the press. If someone saw you at the airport there are going to be reporters up there. Are you ready for all that? Just asking, okay?"

Another thing I had learned about myself is that right after I shut down and internalize, I tend to get tough. Listen to me psychoanalyzing myself. Well, if that is not the root of poetry, then I don't know what is. I stopped sniffling. I stopped the little girl act and moved into the brave phase.

"I deal with that stuff all the time, Owen. I just hate to bring it home with me."

"Hey, anything you bring home is okay as long as it is attached to you. We love you, girl."

I flashed my best smile. "I called Joan Evert from Stompe Publishing and she is going to come up here and deflect the press if it gets too bad. She was with me in Kenya and she knows what I know. She'll be at the Holiday Inn in Fondy. Everything that comes near Ghost Farm will be funneled off to her. As you recall, she is good at what she does. And she is a good friend, too."

"I remember her. Awesome."

"So I will deal with Mom and Joan will take care of everything else."

"Sounds good to me."

I could see Owen shifting gears into a more relaxed mode. Me, too. I soft-punched his shoulder.

"So what is new with you guys, besides Melanie's baby coming?"

"Well, we have that movie crew in town..."

"Oh, yeah. How is that going?"

"Well, the director pesters Molly a bit, but I think she really likes the attention."

I am not sure what else Owen and I talked about on the way home. We got stuck in a traffic backup due to an accident near the split off between Routes 41 and 45, which caused us to veer off into countryside skirting the Kettle Moraine. The Kettle, or Kettles, as the locals refer to the area is an unexpected preview of the Wisconsin wilderness that mostly lies farther to the north. It is glacier trail country; the location of many of my hikes and nature outings as a kid. As we rolled into Kewaskum, I made a sentimental request.

"Wanna slide up to Jersey Flats?"

Owen glanced over to me with a smile flickering on the corner of his mouth.

"You remember that place, huh?"

"Of course. It is the place where you and Mom finally hooked up. Everyone's going to know that after the movie comes out."

"I suppose you're right," Owen mumbled and we left Route 45 for the county roads that led to that special place. I had already called Mom twice on this ride and I called her once more to tell her where we were and why we would be a little late. She said she was about to light up the coals so I'm glad I stalled her a bit. When we got to Jersey Flats I wanted to go just a bit farther to the country store in New Prospect. I had always been fascinated by the inventory of curios, local goods in jars, and bygone atmosphere and I needed some goofy gifts for some people. This place never let me down. There were some film trucks parked across the road at the supper club and Owen told me he thought the movie crew was shooting there later. I was more interested in the store.

I couldn't be sure if the old lady behind the counter was the same old lady from when I was younger, but she did look familiar, as though she had not moved an inch in ten years. She looked up as we walked in and nodded, quickly returning her eyes to the newspaper she was reading.

I bought a ceramic Last Supper, some faded note cards with a blue jay theme, and a Kessler's Whiskey shot glass. Owen got two jars of apple butter. We paid next to nothing for our purchases, but I think we made the day of the old lady just by stopping in. In the car we took inventory.

"The Last Supper?"

"Yeah, I had never seen that one before. And a Kessler's shot glass.

"Hah, Vitamin K. Who gets that?"

"Maybe Des…"

Owen had stopped the car across from the kame in the middle of the Flats.

"You still seeing that guy?"

"Well, I don't see him that much, but…let's change the subject okay? You wanna get out and walk to the kame?"

"Honestly, Sony we don't have the time. Your mom is dying to see you. Maybe it's enough to just be here and look."

We both stared at the little treed hill with, I'm sure, very different thoughts. Family legend has it that Owen was up there one day and Mom rode up on a horse and claimed him. I know it's more complicated than that, but something magical happened back then. My thoughts shot off to Des O'Conner. I wish we had a romantic story beyond what everyone in the world thought they knew and maybe we did. We just did not have the ending that Mom and Owen had. We never would. Des and I had climbed our share of hills in Ireland and I wondered what would happen if I could get him up this one

"You ready to go home?" Owen asked breaking off my reverie.

I smiled so hard my cheek hurt. "Jah, let's go home."

CHAPTER SEVEN

BIM

My life is changing right before my eyes. We all like a certain comfortable routine we can count on to help sort out the day, but what do you do when it all goes into the crapper? I allowed myself two beers this morning and decided that it is much better to swim than to sink. That, my friends, is why beer is good for you. It gives perspective. First you deal with the minor things. I let the newspaper give me a laptop computer. It seems Pat already had wi-fi in the house so I get a pretty good signal out here in the garage. If I am sounding like I understand all of this, I don't. I am just telling you what they are telling me. So, I am connected to the world and beginning to explore it a little each day. Of course, the paper wants my column emailed to them so writing on the machine and the things you have to do to email were my first lessons.

As I mentioned before I am mostly one-handed these days. I peck out letters and they appear on the screen. Crude, but easy enough. Then this kid from the paper shows me the rest of it: a four day lesson that had me ready to use my one good hand to strangle him. In the end, here I am, Bim Stouffer, garage sitter and web surfer. Joining the cyber world was the least of my problems.

Pat had her first chemo therapy last week and her hair is coming out in clumps. Molly and her shopped for a wig, which I actually like, but I hate what it is masking. Not the baldness, but the symptoms of the illness and treatment. Pat handles it well, I must say. She goes off to the clinic like she is going to war: determined and brave. Well, she is sick as a dog for a couple days and I worry because I can't really take care of her in a physical way. So the next big change comes along. I was in the garage trying to think of what to write in my column this week when Pat comes out the backdoor with that look; the one that tells me I am about to be informed about something I have no control over.

"Hi, honey. You got a minute?" she said and she plunked down beside me.

"I got hours, Patsy. What's up?"

There was a long pause before the 'well' so I knew I'd better brace myself.

"Well, how would you feel about having some company?"

Now it was my turn to pause. Company was not so bad, but it never got this much set up before. "Who's coming over?"

"Actually…" Not my favorite word. "Actually, Carrie and Mike are going to come and live here for a while."

So it was houseguests instead of company. My brain, though stroked a bit, works much faster than the rest of me so I was able to add it all up in an instant. Pat needed help and her daughter, Carrie had not been home for ages. That might work pretty well, but I could not picture Mr. Hot Shot Photographer sitting in the garage with me for any extended period of time. Don't get me wrong, I love Carrie and think Mike Gabler is a great guy, but I didn't think little Fond du Lac fit their lifestyles anymore.

"And they agreed to this?" I asked.

"Carrie came up with the idea."

"That figures. And Mike? "

"Mike is more like you than you know, but he signed off anyway."

I winced at the backhanded compliment. "Well, that sounds a little…"

Pat cut me off. "That sounds a little like a family pulling together, Bim. I know you don't care for company or any kind of change, but I need someone to help out around here until I am done with all of this treatment stuff. Carrie wants to be here to help us when I can't. You get that, right? You men will roll with it, okay?"

I could see this was a done deal and it made sense. Anyway, my days of loud protest were long over. Besides, I love my wife more than I love my routine or anything else for that matter. I took her hand.

"Should be some interesting garage talk with Super Mike filling me in on how he is photographing all those Hollywood starlets and rock and rollers."

"Honey, you will have your garage to yourself most of the time. Mike will not be here every day, but they will be based out of here until the end of the year. Four months from now I plan on being cancer free. How's that for incentive?"

"When do they arrive?"

"In about four days. Next Saturday."

"I'm good."

Pat squeezed my hand. "How many beers did you sneak this morning?"

"A couple-a two."

"That's it for today," she said as she headed back to the house. She was right. I had some clear thinking to do.

I just emailed my column off to the paper. We have a mid-term election coming up in November and it is never too soon to expose the crooks on both sides as the lies begin to pile up in early September. I was astounded by how dumb these guys think we are until I thought it over. We are dumb. But, while I was doing a little research I kept stumbling on articles about the youngest Costello girl, Sonia. Every time I typed 'Fond du Lac' into the search bar, her name popped up.

It seems someone took a potshot at her over in Africa. That's upsetting. I have known Sonia for years since she was a girl and have followed her rise to celebrity status just like everyone else in town. When Pat's grandson and Sonia's sister married she became family over here. Now, I know she was adopted by Molly, who was adopted by Roland, but the girl somehow got the writing genes from both of them. I may not be much of a poetry expert, but I'd say little Sony sure can write verse. Wait a second, I'll find you an example:

Watercolor words are whispered
Across moody lands where ground fog hugs
The prairie grasses mowed by giants who
Had married up the fairies of the kame
Their children all had granite eyes and
Limestone hearts and the holy glacier ghost
Baptized them in His name

Like I said, the kid can write. So why is someone always kidnapping her or shooting at her? Maybe my garage is too far away from the craziness of this world. Maybe that is why I like to sit here and watch the birds in the trees and my wife in the kitchen window. I wonder sometimes if it is a sin to be so damned safe. Maybe there is an evil in this world that is drawn to goodness. Maybe that is why Pat is sick, but then why would that evil sniff around an old goat like me? Oh shit, I promised myself to never wonder about my stroke or why it happened. I read somewhere (probably Roland) that while we biologicals are soft bags of water our souls are encased in stone. Hey, maybe that is what Sonia was writing about. I think maybe I should interview her for my next column. That would give this town something to talk about besides which crook is going to be voted into an office he or she will then corrupt. Good idea, Bimster!

CHAPTER EIGHT

DESMOND

I arrived in the mythical state of Wisconsin during a thunderstorm. Don't you sometimes question the wisdom of landing a jet on ground that is being struck by lightning and where trees are being shred of their leaves? Well, maybe you do, but strapped in your seat you are in God's hands... somebody's hands. Anyway, we landed and everyone applauded and cheered. I could hear the thunder claps through the fuselage as we docked at the gate. There was some confusion at the car rental desk as they had never seen an international driver's license before. While the girl was waiting for a manager to approve me she kept throwing out names of Irish citizens she was related to and wondering if I knew any of them. I was struck by the warmth of Americans from this outpost, but all the American football references at this airport would have suggested hooliganism in other parts of the world. These Packers, whatever a Packer is, seem to be more popular than God (thank you John Lennon).

I eventually located my car, a Ford with many bells and whistles including, thankfully, a GPS. I programmed Pipe into the system and a pathway magically appeared. I would be heading south mostly, but I got a little distracted before I got far from the airport. There was a casino run by the local Indian tribe that I could not resist.

Lady Luck and I have had even more of an estranged relationship than my wife and I. I don't ever win, but for some reason I love to lose. Losing at games of chance is the one thing in my life that I can expect and count on and so I somehow enjoy that small, poor island of stability. Of course, I can afford to lose a bit here and there. Cedric would tell me that I cannot afford it anymore, but there I was at a black jack table at a place called Oneida, doing my part and losing. The Native American dealer, whose name was Janet, was very pretty and provided two very lovely, dainty hands with which she gathered my chips…endlessly.

I learned there was no alcohol served in the place because it was on the reservation. This neighborhood did not fit my image of an Indian reservation, but what the hell did I know about it? I did know that I have always been fascinated by the aspect of people-watching during the drama of gambling. And I do mean drama in every sense. No where I know is man upon a stage and acting out a part more than in a casino. The fact that this tribe had removed the drinking did not diminish the posturing of winners and losers. Winners frown and losers smile. Body language and gestures are broad, but one must always read them in the reverse of their intentions. A casual wave of the hand and a grin to a loss cloaks a crisis. A slammed fist and a frown means, 'damn, I won again. Sorry!'

When an ATM machine refused my card I called Cedric and he seemed quite pleased about the situation.

"So you found a casino as soon as you landed? How you of you, Desmond."

I so hate that haughty South African accent when used against me.

"Spare me the gaming lecture and put some money in my Visa, if you don't mind." I didn't want to sound like I was pleading, but being in America without money is indeed frightening.

"How much do you need?"

"What can I get?"

This was an old cat and mouse game. I understand that part of Ced's job is to force my frugality, but I always bristle over the control he has. "I could use five thousand dollars, American."

"Hmmm…," he began, "that used to be a modest request, but as of late that seems a tad high."

I waited without saying a word. I watched Janet's shift come to an end replacing her with a brute I had no intention of sitting across from. I could hear Cedric typing something into his computer.

"I just made a transfer to your card. Des, you have to make this 5K last, okay?"

"It's really that bad?"

"Worse. Listen, I have an idea. Why don't you call the folks at Stompe in Boston and see if they can set up a book signing appearance or two while you are in the States. Wisconsin used to buy a lot of your books. Raise some cash for a change instead of spending it."

"Good idea, but I am not sure I even have a friend over there since Harry died and my agent quit."

"Try it. Give them a call. It can't hurt. Tell them where you are and that you are writing another book of love poems to your little American friend. They might see some profit in that since this latest incident."

That bit of information made my heart stop. "What latest incident?"

"Just hit the paper here today. 'American poet and celebrity Sonia Costello was treated for a gunshot wound in Nairobi last week.' It goes on to say she was just slightly injured, treated and released, and no other details are available as yet."

"Jaysus, Ced. Does it say where she is now?"

"No, but where would you go if you were shot?"

"Home?"

"My guess is that you and she are not that far apart. Why don't you leave the casino and find her?"

Cedric, I swear, is my better self. He had just given me my mission and I was anxious to begin to get to it. I now couldn't wait to get down the road. We signed off and I once again pointed my rental south. I tried an old phone number that I had for Sonia with a 920 area code. I got an answering machine with Molly's voice and left a short message. I then turned my attention to the GPS. The robotic female voice of the GPS began her directions: "Turn left and proceed south on Oneidea Boulevard…"

It was dark by the time I got out of Green Bay and began to head down to Pipe. It was a warm night with lingering lightning on the distant horizon. I fancied the very air crackling with the electricity of my quest. Hah, that romantic notion dissipated with each gruesome road kill that I dodged along the way. I was astounded by the apparent suicidal tendencies of the local raccoons and opossums. Like doomed lovers, they seemed to die in pairs. The doomed lovers theme began to depress me. I recalled for the thousandth time how I met and fell in love with for Sonia Costello.

Harry Stompe, a wonderful man and father figure to me, used to be the editor for a literary magazine, *Art Harvest*. I was first attracted to Harry's magazine because of his great articles about Roland Heinz. Heinz was a sensation in Ireland. He was heralded as the American Joyce and his two Pulitzer books were required reading for not only aspiring novelists, but poets alike. I would pour myself a stiff drink, settle into an easy chair, and dive into *A Winter Light* and *The Tap Root*. I had no experience, besides Joyce with such prosaic intimacy and beauty. When *The Needle's Eye* arrived, I began to flood *Art Harvest* with poems inspired by Heinz. Harry Stompe saw the Roland influence in my work and published me two or three times and soon after I became a regular contributor. I began to build a following.

I should say here that having the profession of an Irish poet is not quite as ridiculous as it sounds. There is a tradition of poets in Ireland. It is respectable. In fact almost everyone is a poet of some sort. A priest reads the liturgy like the poem it is. A drunk waxes aloud to his mates about his life in the most poetic terms. A person who loves another could find no greater way to express it than in a poem spoken in Gaelic. I am proud of my gift, but often ashamed of the way I use it. Getting paid so much to create so little is a sin. I confess it. But, when the money was offered as it was by Harry Stompe, my ego kept the change. Besides, all the guilt and rot, it is my only talent.

When Harry took his next step and founded Stompe Publishing Company he took me with him. Together we crafted a plan for three books of my poems to be translated internationally and sales, to both our surprise, were quite decent. Then, as they say, fate stepped into the picture. Harry was cultivating another younger poet from Wisconsin and this girl was no less than Roland Heinz's adopted granddaughter. Harry introduced me to her at a meet-and-greet in Boston just after her release from her captives in Darfur. I was prepared to meet what I thought was my competition, but I quickly forgot about all that when we shook hands. It was not the handshake, but the eye contact that did me in. I was instantly lost in those dark, smiling pools of intelligence and vulnerability. In that moment my heart flew away, my marriage virtually ended, my creativity surged, and my very skin no longer seemed to be holding me together.

It is so hard to describe this sort of thing. I still ponder it daily. With all the people on this planet how can just one of them change your life with a smile? It was not so much love at first sight as total fascination. I could not take my eyes off of her the rest of the evening.

I remember Molly getting me alone and beginning a strange conversation.

"Hello, Mr. O'Conner," she said, "I don't know if you remember me. I'm Molly Costello."

Molly Costello and I had met a few years earlier at another one of Harry's parties. I vaguely remembered probing her about all things Roland. Anyway, it was before Sony's kidnapping and before I was even aware there was a daughter poet in the Costello family. Anything I could learn about my idol, Roland Heinz was pure gold for me back then. I even did an interview for her about my interest in her father as it applied to my poetry. It was an interview she conducted on line so our personal connection was never that strong

"I do indeed remember you, Molly. How are you?" I asked. Now Molly has a dazzling smile, also, but I found myself looking past it to her daughter. Molly made me focus on her instantly.

"Hey!"

"I'm sorry?" Her friendly tone changed quickly to one with a point like an icicle stiletto.

"Hey, Irish. Surely you recognize one of your own? And I don't mean my daughter. She's got my last name, but as you can see, she is not one of us so can we talk frankly?"

I had not realized how obvious my staring had been. Molly had. Now, there was a little twinkle in her eye, like she might be bluffing or jesting a bid, but I decided to try to take control with a wee bit of Irish bullshit.

"She writes like she's Irish."

"You've been staring a hole in her all night. She hasn't noticed, but I have."

"And you're protecting her from what, Irish poets, Ms. Costello?"

She took my elbow and led me to a quiet spot. I was mostly amused. Molly Costello is also a beautiful woman and I had already spoken to her date, a charming doctor of some sort with some nasty facial scars. I wondered what she was going to say to me.

"Can I call you, Desmond?" she asked in almost a whisper.

"Make it Des."

"Okay, Des. Listen, I'm sorry. I am not trying to hover over my daughter like a mother hen. I would have been appalled if my mother had done that to me. But, I do know what the aftermath of a thunderbolt looks like and you have it."

"I do?" Of course, I knew I did. I could still smell the ozone.

"Yes, and I see a married man who just got a strong notion."

"How do you know…?"

"Your bio, Des." She tapped a rolled up program for the evening against my chest. "I wrote a story on you once. Do you even remember that?"

"Well, excuse me…can I call you Molly? I have done nothing except admire Sonia from afar. I reserve that right even though married. I am a man with two very good eyes. As for that interview, it was forgettable." God, how awful that sounds even now as I type it a few years later. I think we both had had a little too much champagne.

At that point Owen, her partner, lover, whatever came over. I think he had seen her strike me with the program and decided to see if a referee was needed. Molly introduced us.

"Owen Palmer, this is Desmond O'Conner, the famous poet."

My head cocked at 'famous.'

"We already met at the bar," said I.

I had immediately liked this guy, especially when I learned later he was an animal doctor. We shook hands once more and that act alone seemed to end the tension.

"Molly was just reciting some of my poetry back to me."

Owen slipped his arm around Molly. "Actually, it looked to me like she was getting between you and another poet."

I felt cornered and used the old last ditch Irish defense: honesty...sort of.

"Look, she's talented and she has a light around here. Surely you can see how I would be..."

Molly cut me off again. In Owen's grasp she felt her own honesty escaping. "Stop. Des, you don't need to go on. I apologize for insinuating anything. These occasions, here among all of Harry's clients make me crazy. The truth is I...we are huge fans of your writing."

She looked at Owen as she spoke and he nodded to me. Molly continued.

"I am trying to learn how to not be jealous of my daughter's talent and charm. I had been looking for an opening to approach you about your recent poetry and I kept seeing you staring at her. I wanted you to sign these books for me." Owen held out two books that I had no trouble identifying as my own.

"We love your writing, Des. These books sit on our bedside table," she said.

The picture that leapt into my mind of those books next to their bed was my most vivid glimpse into the relationship between writer and reader. Molly and Owen became my friends right there, although I would test that friendship in the months ahead. I signed their books as though I was signing a contract with the Costellos. Molly knew that what she had just said was to disarm me and make me focus on my intentions. I knew this instinctively, too. I knew that she also knew I was not going to just disappear back to Ireland and my wife, who still remains nameless. We both knew it was chapter one of a new book. I began chapter two the next day.

My reverie ended with a feeling of great fatigue. After all, I had been traveling for almost the last two days. I stopped and let the GPS suggest a local hotel. I found only one with a vacancy, but it was in Fond du Lac. I passed through Pipe and was not much impressed with what amounted to a few houses, a couple bars, and a gas station. I decided rest was more important than investigation so I probably drove right past Sonia in the darkness.

The Holiday Inn parking lot was filled with film trucks, which struck me as odd. I heard some loud carousing coming from the lounge as I registered, but as I said, I was too tired for anything social. I sleepwalked to my room.

CHAPTER NINE

MOLLY

It was a long day already when Sony and Owen got back to Ghost Farm. Yeah, I saw the bandage first and my daughter second. I operate like that sometimes. The fact was, while I was beyond happy to have my youngest home and safe, I was flat out pissed off that someone might have tried to kill her. This rage surprised me and almost ruined the evening. Almost. Owen knows my moods and easily defeats the bad ones. He quickly opened a bottle of good wine that we had been saving and made a toast to Sony being home. I took a sip, a deep breath, and came in out of left field.

"So, honey, anything interesting happen in Africa this time?" I said it with a smile and a spontaneous giggle.

"Not much, Mom, another day, another bullet."

Graveyard humor has always been big at Ghost Farm. I drifted away from my inquisition and allowed the evening to take its course. We were at the old picnic table near the back door and the summer stars were popping out above the oak tree. It was still over 80 degrees, but a breeze had come up off the lake that was promising. While Owen took Sonia out to his office to look at some new puppies, I went in the house to check the answering machine. I had expected a call from Jon about a script meeting in the morning. What I found was a mumbled message from Des O'Conner. He was in Wisconsin and looking for Sonia. My mood once again soured.

"What's wrong, Mom? You were fine before we went out to the barn and now you act like you're angry again."

The wine and I decided to tell the truth. "There was a message on the machine from Des."

This item of news hung in the humid air and seemed to hum at the same frequency as the cicadas. Des is the bad penny who keeps turning up from time to time and he usually causes Sony some pain. How could he not? He is still married and still fourteen or fifteen years older than my daughter. Not a good combination. And yes, I know he looks like he could be Owen's little brother. It all adds up to heartache.

"What did he say?"

"Only that he was coming into town, had heard the news about your...incident, and he wanted to speak to you."

"It figures he would have heard about that," Owen said nodding to the bandage, "and called. But, I wonder what he is doing here in Wisconsin?"

I could tell Sonia didn't like Owen and me discussing Des and his intentions. I do respect her decisions and privacy. It's her life for cry-eye.

"Did he leave a number?" Sony asked in a faked tone of not caring all that much.

"Yes. You want it? It's still on the machine."

"I'll get it later."

That was the end of it; or the beginning. We went on to talk about Melanie and her baby and how neat it was that she wanted to have the child born here at the farm. I was picturing an incredible family Christmas, but it seemed a long way off. We had some summer left, then the fall, maybe an Indian Summer, and then (dare I even write the word?) winter.

Just then the phone rang again and we all heard it because I had taken the cordless house phone outside with me. There was no caller I.D. on this relic of another age.

"Do you want me to answer it?" I put the question to Sony.

"Go ahead. It's not his ring," she said. Owen smiled.

It was Jon Greenwood wondering about a breakfast meeting at the Holiday Inn. I knew Owen would be working to catch up for his day off today so I accepted. As an afterthought I asked if I could bring my daughter. I knew that everyone on that crew would recognize Sonia so I was sort of trumping the cast's star power with some of my own. Jon loved the idea.

"Is that okay with you?" I asked Sony. She smiled and nodded.

"Okay, we'll be there. 7AM. Okay, bye, Jon."

Later, Sonia crashed on the couch while watching the news and I didn't have the heart to wake her to go up to bed. She knew the way if she woke up. Anyway, it was time for Owen and I to have a pow-wow before we slept. I always had to catch myself when I came out of the bathroom and found him in my big old bed, the one the old farmers left with the ghosts under it. He was reading, as he often did before sleep, and the soft glow of the lamp next to him made his face even more handsome. It was warm outside even at 11 PM, but it was damned hot in the bedroom. The heat of the day rose to the second floor and stayed there smoldering. I switched on the oscillating fan on the dresser and got into bed.

I snuggled into Owen and he put the book on his stomach. "I'm glad she is home," he whispered.

"Oh my god, yes. She crashed on the couch. Poor thing is exhausted."

"Honey, you did say Des was in Wisconsin, right?"

I had almost forgotten about Des. "That's what he said."

"He certainly has a sense of timing."

"Bad timing."

Owen was quiet for a moment and I thought I knew what he was thinking, but he surprised me.

"Molly, have you ever thought there is any possibility that Des was the one who paid that ransom?"

"Huh?"

"Well, I was thinking, he knew you before the kidnapping, right? He had the Roland and Stompe connections, too. He had that kind of money back then and maybe he was on the kidnapper's list of people to hit up."

I had never considered this notion. I had always felt deep down that the government had paid Sonia's ransom out of some sort of slush fund. Since no one had ever come forward, it seemed like the only logical answer. Back then I didn't really care who had gotten her release, but now my brain began to swirl.

"How would the kidnapper contact Des? It all happened so fast. She was only missing for a week and I don't think Des O'Conner operates that fast on any level. It was another corner of the world. He could not have been involved, honey."

"Well, it's something to think about it. Sony has never talked much about her own theories, has she?"

"No," I said. This was opening old wounds and I did not like it before bed, but I had always been curious about how things had come down back then.

"Well, babe, since he's in town maybe we could just ask him?"

"I have a feeling he is not going to be around here for long and you or I contacting him is going to piss off Sony." I scooted up on the pillow so I could look right at Owen. "I am not sure I want to know anymore about the kidnapping or who ransomed her. We got a good outcome and some things may need to remain a secret. The shooting thing is something else, but no more tonight. Okay?"

Owen smiled as he reached for the light. The room went dark. "Just thinkin' out loud. You're right. Goodnight, sweetie."

We kissed in the dark.

In the morning when I came down the stairs, Sonia was already up and on the phone although apparently not with Desmond. I found the coffee already made and half the pot gone. I poured a cup and it was Sonia's brew alright, much stronger than I make it. She came through the kitchen door looking very awake and mildly annoyed.

"Morning, Sony. What's up?"

She plunked down across from me and put her chin on her knuckles. "That was Joan Evert on the phone. She got in last night and is over at the Holiday Inn in Fond du Lac. She is already taking calls from The FBI and State Department about Nairobi."

"Oh?"

"Mom, the good news is that they are only semi-interested. If I was killed they might be more concerned, she said. The bad news is because the film crew is in town, the paparazzi is already here following Sarah Dylan. I got a feeling we may be having some unwanted company crawling around the farm."

I had a caffeinated moment. "Hey, why not just hold a press conference at the hotel and disarm them? Let them take some pictures and pass their attention back over to Sarah?"

I was thinking out loud into my coffee cup, but when I looked up I saw a big smile on Sonia's face.

"Mom, that is a great idea!"

"It is?"

"Yeah, Joan can set it up for later today. We are already going over there for breakfast. Sarah will be there, too. We'll give them a photo op before they start googling maps to Ghost Farm. It's a super idea. I need to call Joan back."

Sony sprinted back into the living room to put the wheels in motion. I had a moment to think about what was going to happen. Was this the way celebrities operated? Seizing moments and predicting the behavior of the press? Was Sonia really that famous?

Well, as a protective mother, I had sort of thought some of her luster had worn off and I was afraid that she would not stand up to Sarah Dylan's star shine. I got a real dose of pop culture reality later that day at the Holiday Inn.

CHAPTER TEN

DESMOND

My first day in Fond du Lac, Wisconsin was first busy and then eventful. I awakened at the Holiday Inn frozen stiff. I had switched on the air-conditioner to full blast before bed and was too tired to adjust it during the night. I leapt from bed and opened the drapes to assure myself that it was still summer and snow had not fallen overnight. I looked out expectantly to perhaps see some woods or a lake, but my view took in only a busy freeway. The town was no where in sight. I shut down the cooler and my phone rang instantly. I saw it was Cedric. I had slept until noon local time so it was evening in Ireland.

"Cedric, good day to you."

"Hello, Des. How is America today?"

Hah, his first order of business was to remind me where I was. Not a bad idea actually. "America is fine. What's up, old boy?"

I heard Ced sigh. Now what?

"Please don't hate me, Desmond, but I did make a call to Stompe Publishing earlier today. I spoke to a...let me see (shuffling papers), a Mr. Scott. Adam Scott. I explained to him that I am your agent and..."

"You're my what?"

"Don't get upset. I am your default agent these days, am I not?"

"Go on," I said as I rubbed my free hand through my tangled hair.

"Bear with me. I informed Mr. Scott that you were in Wisconsin and working on a new collection of poems."

"Did this man even know who I am?"

"Yes, Des, of course he knows who you are. You are still a part of the Stompe family."

"Okay." I took the mobile into the bathroom so I could relieve myself. This call was getting interesting though ill-timed.

"Scott is a smart man, Des, and he quickly linked your trip to Ms. Costello. I think he realized that if you and she were to be connected again that your poems might once again be marketable."

"He told you that?"

"Yes, and he was quite specific about it. He told me that if you could come up with a fresh collection accompanied by some new photos of you and Sonia Costello that it might put you back on track with them."

"Did you ask for an advance?"

"Of course. That, my friend, is why I called. That's what an agent does. God knows you weren't going to make that call."

"How much?"

"Well, here's the deal."

I flushed and returned to the window for the terms of the deal.

"Mr. Scott is going to set you up with some local events over there that you must attend. He wants some new poems submitted and a few photos in the meantime. If you can follow up quickly with the submissions and do the book events promoting the old and the new, he can advance you $10,000."

"I could get that much from the yellow press for just photos of me and her."

"Perhaps, but would you rather be a poet or a paparazzi shill, Desmond?"

Of course, those words galvanized me. I was absolutely nothing if not a poet.

"Do you know when the first book event is happening?"

"It will take a week or so to set things up. If I were you I would start writing. Any inspiration yet?"

"Cedric, I just woke up, opened the drapes, and peed."

"You used to be able to turn that into a poem, Des."

I nodded to no one. He had me starting to focus again. The man was amazing.

"Okay, I hear you loud and clear. This project is going to take some time. I don't even know the lay of the land yet. And I can't stay in this hotel. There is a film crew here and it is distracting and noisy."

"I already thought of that."

"Of course, you did. What?"

"I have been searching rentals for you in the Fond du Lac area. I found a house in the country, just like you always prefer. And, here's the kicker, old man: I found a cheap old farmhouse in Pipe. Isn't that where Ms. Costello is from?"

"She used to be. I suppose her Mom still lives around there somewhere. Who do I see about this place?"

"Do you have internet access at this hotel?"

"Of course."

"Well, switch on your computer and all the contact information is already in an email to you. I also sent you the contact info from Stompe Publishing. Make a couple follow up phone calls today and your writing career could be instantly resurrected."

I was starting to wake up now and details were flooding my brain. "And I suppose you think that since you are now my agent you are getting five per cent of me?"

"I was actually thinking eight per cent was more in line. After all, before today you were getting one hundred per cent of nothing."

"Let's negotiate after I get some coffee."

"Make the calls, Des. Get it going again. Oh, and by the way, your girl is definitely in Wisconsin. I am on the Stompe emailing list now and the first one I got was detailing a Sonia Costello press conference for this evening at 5PM your time."

"And where might that be?"

"It says, Holiday Inn, Fond du Lac, Wisconsin."

The following adrenaline rush triggered by surprise and fear made my need for coffee useless. I got off the phone and suddenly felt like fate had dropped me off in the middle of either a big crisis or a bigger joke. Of course, it could be Cupid pulling the strings, but that was more of a wish. I showered and called the local realtor about the house. Nothing fancy she said; an abandoned farm house on the ledge, whatever that was. I got the information and made a date to meet her here and we'd drive up to what she referred to as the old Bollander place.

Have you ever been in a situation that seemed so strange that it could not be coincidence or even chaotic? As I pondered how I ended up at the same hotel that Sonia was going to use for a press conference later I had to try to back up my memory as to how all of the dominoes began to fall for this to happen. I did not know she had been shot at when I left Limerick for America, so rescue was not in play. I really did not expect her to be around here so confronting her was not a motivation. I had allowed the GPS to find a hotel so even the human factor had been removed. It was in the shower that I surrendered to kismet and began to understand my part in my own story. I was in love and, being a writer, I needed to find the source of my creative fountain and drink heavily from it. Of course, I ended up at the bar at hotel lounge in pursuit of my metaphor.

I was waiting for the realtor, a Julie Kleinbach, to meet me and drive me out to inspect the rental. I had pretty much already decided to take the place no matter what condition it was in because I really didn't care what condition it was in. I only needed a place to write and maybe hide out for a while. It was about two in the afternoon and the bar was mostly empty. The film crew was out somewhere doing what they do and I was curious about what they were filming. I decided to ask the bartender and before she could answer someone sat down beside me and began to fill me in. I felt the tingle of electricity before I even turned to face her. I would recognize Sarah Dylan anywhere, even if it was completely unexpected to see her in at a bar in Wisconsin.

"The film is called *Holyland* and it is based on the book by Molly Costello. She's from around here," Ms. Dylan stated. I think my mouth was still hanging open.

"I, I know that book," I stammered. "I even know Molly Costello."

Sarah is a smart lady with a quick mind. I could tell she was digesting not only my information, but my Irish accent and my face.

"I know who you are," she said with an amazing smile.

"And I know you, too."

"Hi, I'm Sarah and you are Desmond O'Conner." She looked around the room as if trying to locate someone else. "I had breakfast with Sonia today."

Ah, the power of the press. My affair with Sonia was so well documented that even self-absorbed Hollywood types had followed it. It never ceased to amaze me how big the appetite for scandal was. Of course, Sarah Dylan had her own romances documented in the tabloids so we met on even ground. I relaxed a bit as I sipped a beer. The bartender brought Sarah one, too

"Nice to meet you, Sarah. And well, Sonia does not know I'm here In fact, I barely know I am here myself. Sorry, it's a rather long story...even for an Irishman "

A half hour later, both our stories had been shared. She had the afternoon off from the shoot, but had to go back to work that evening. When my realtor lady showed up, wide-eyed at meeting Sarah, I had to go myself. Julie Kleinbach was also a rather attractive woman, but I was star-struck by Sarah on one hand and love-struck by Sonia on the other. I was eager to find my new hideout if only to reorganize my priorities. And begin to write about them, too.

The old Bollander place sat on high ground above Lake Winnebago that the locals referred to as The Ledge. As we pulled onto the property I was struck by the amazing view and expanse of the huge body of water. I was surprised by the beauty. The house on the other hand, was quite run down. Before we went inside Julie explained to me how the owner had moved away several years ago and not much had been done as far as upkeep was concerned. This was even more apparent when we went inside. There were animal droppings on the kitchen floor and an odor of must and rot. In other words it looked and smelled much like the place I had grown up in. I almost expected me mum to be boiling potatoes in the kitchen and me da to be drunk in the parlor. I knew and understood this place and instantly loved it.

"I'm sorry for the condition of the house," Julie said. "I had no idea it was this bad out here." She was clearly embarrassed, but I put her at ease at once.

"Ah, Julie, then you have never been to Ireland. It is not all quaintness and fresh paint. I'll take this place. When can I move in?"

"You're sure, Mr. O'Conner?"

"Yes, yes, very sure."

"Well, I can have someone come out to clean tomorrow and we can sign the papers then. That sound okay?"

"Well, actually, I would like to take it as is and move in today. Is that possible?"

"Well, I guess so. We do need to go back to my office and do the paper work. I will need a security deposit and first months rent, too." She paused and looked around. "Are you sure you want to live here?"

I had walked into the living room and was taking in the view. "I am very sure. In fact this house is perfect for me. Is there a term lease? Any restrictions to a foreign lessor?"

"No restrictions that I know of," she said, "but there is at least a six month lease that you will have to sign."

"Not a problem."

We drove back to Fond du Lac; I signed a lease that I might or might not honor, paid cash for the fees, and took the key. I checked out of the Holiday Inn before the press conference. There was no way I was going to get caught dead there in the costume of a stalker. Of course, I had no idea at that time that the location of my new rental was well within a stalker's range. The old Bollander place, as I found out, was right above the Costello farm down on Highway 151. Oh, how the fates must have gibbered amongst themselves as they saw me wander into their snare. There were more surprises ahead, of course, but for that first night I was content to sit in a musty easy chair, drink a half a bottle of Jameson, and sleep the sleep of an expatriate Irishman in America's Dairyland.

CHAPTER ELEVEN

BIM

I got a call from Reinholt at the paper asking me how well I knew Sonia Costello. Of course, I played it up big how we were old friends and how close our families were. Turns out he wanted me to go to a press conference at the Holiday Inn that Sony was having later that day. I had zero interest in leaving the garage on such a fine day to go over to a dreary hotel to see little Sonia get blitzed by the press. Especially, if they expected me to be a member of that press. In my mind, my role was merely that of an observer. *Bim's Garage* was local interest, small town crap. I knew that and accepted it. It was a hobby for cry-eye. But, then I had to somehow back up my bragging so I told him I would run over there and see if they would let me in the place. Pat wasn't around so I called a cab. One thing you never want to do is call a cab in a town like this one. They should call it thugs on wheels.

I can get around okay as long as I use one of those walkers. I personally hate the contraption, but it works as a prop to keep me from falling and then it converts into a nice portable chair. I also noticed that when people see you coming in with a walker they generally smile benignly and let you pass. Wheel chairs get bigger smiles and wider berths, but who wants that?

I got my sullen cabbie to drop me off and I shuffled into the hotel. Lots of action there, but it wasn't all for Sony. Some of the local groupies and busy-bodies were hanging around trying to get a picture or an autograph from a movie star. It was chaos in the lobby until I spotted someone I knew.

"Hey Owen," I yelled and my favorite veterinarian came over smiling.

"What the hell are you doing here, Bim?"

"Good question. Good to see you, Owen." We shook hands. "I have been assigned to cover our girl's press conference for the local rag. You got any idea of how I am supposed to do that?"

Owen is a good guy—the best. When he and Molly hooked up we sort of became buddies through our women. Them being best friends and all. I also suspected he was a better doctor than the one I went to regularly. At least his clients left with a biscuit.

"Let me see, Bim. I think you need to register with the gal who's acting as Sony's agent. She's at that table over there and her name is Joan. She will give you a badge or something and you can go into the meeting room."

"Yeah, okay, but what is this all about?"

"Well, Sonia is trying to defuse the story about that shooting incident in Africa before it spreads to the farm. We are all looking for some quiet time and privacy."

"She still attracts all this attention, Owen?"

"It seems she does. Of course, having a film crew here in town only adds to the circus. That and the fact that they are filming Molly's book. And then, when it can't possibly get more complicated…"

"Yeah?"

"I heard Des O'Conner is in town, too."

Now there was a name I hadn't heard in a while. "No shit, that crazy Irishman is back on the scene? I thought he and Sony were kaput."

"Maybe they are. Who knows?"

"You know, Doc, I can remember this town when the biggest news story was that a bridge was built over the railroad tracks on Johnson Street. Now we got movie stars and famous poets milling about grabbing headlines. Roland would roll over in his grave…if he had one."

Owen gave me what I thought was the old coot look. After all I am one. He surprised me.

"You still think about Roland, huh? Me, too and I never even met the man. In a way he started all this didn't he? His fame kind of dragged everyone else along with it."

"Hey, Roland wasn't famous until he was damned near dead. And even then no one knew him around here except for a few old timers."

"Like you."

"Yep, like me. Anyway, maybe he would get a kick out all this fuss."

"Maybe he would."

We both surveyed the bustling lobby.

"Naw, he'd hate it," I said. "So do I. Let's get this over with and I'll buy you a beer, Doc.

"Okay, Bim. I'll get you a seat in front." And he did.

Owen drove me home after the event and I had been writing my story for about forty minutes in the garage when Pat came home. I could tell she had done some shopping in preparation for Carrie and Mike's arrival because the bags were from Home Depot.

"What ya got there, Patsy?" I asked as I closed the laptop.

"Well, I got some new lamp shades for the kids' room."

"What was wrong with the old ones?"

"They were yellow with age. We needed new ones, anyway. What have you been up to all day? I stopped by here before and you were gone."

"I left you a voice message."

"Oh, never got it," she said as she pulled out her mobile phone. "I see it now."

"And you weren't worried about me then?"

"Well, no. I knew you wouldn't get far," she said with a devilish grin. "Besides, I spoke to Molly and she said Owen saw you at the Holiday Inn. How did that thing go?"

I was always amazed at the communication network between Pat and her friends.   "It was nutso, is what it was. I just got done writing about it for the paper. Jack actually asked me to go over there like I am some sort of reporter for god's sake."

Pat pulled up a chair and plunked herself down. "Read it to me, Bim."

I opened the laptop (I am getting more adept at this thing) and read to her:

Several days ago something happened in Nairobi, Kenya that ended up causing a stir right here in Fond du Lac, Wisconsin. How does such a thing happen? Well, when some goofball takes a potshot at our own little local poet, Sonia Costello, it gives us pause and then outrage. We don't hunt poets in Wisconsin, although if they had antlers we probably would. Now Sonia is an old friend of mine and she and I have shared some interesting conversations right here in Bim's Garage. So I asked her what the heck was going on over there in Africa. She told me and the other so-called reporters who had gathered at the Holiday Inn today that she had no idea who took that shot. She also told us that it was probably a random bullet that was not meant for her. I guess those sort of things happen all the time over there. She also told us she was home for a visit with her family and would appreciate it if we (meaning those other goofballs) would leave her alone and respect her privacy. She then introduced Sarah Dylan, a pretty Hollywood actress who went on to plug her movie that they have been shooting around town here. It was a slick hand-off on Sonia's part, but…

"But what, Bim?" Pat asked.

"That's all I got so far. Maybe that is all I will have."

"But, you can't leave it dangling like that. Jack won't like it."

"Patsy, don't get me going about what Jack will like or won't like. I don't give a shit what he likes. Anyway, he don't pay me enough for me to get personal about my friends and their families. And yeah, Sonia did not convince me that nothing much happened to her, but I don't think anyone else got it or cared much once the movie star hit the podium. Sony and Owen slipped out the back and that was that."

"But, if you send that piece you wrote in you will create your own mystery."

"If I send it in."

"You mean you won't?"

"Oh, I'll fix it up some and send it in. Add some fluff about the flat beer and stale nuts at the Holiday Inn bar. That's my job. The other stuff is for The Inquirer or whoever the heck else was looking for dirt out there. What's for dinner?"

We ended up having scalloped potatoes and ham. My favorite. After dinner I wrote a piece of crap for Jack Reinholt, which he loved by the way. Before bed I found myself thinking about Sonia, though. Even my curiosity was piqued by what I didn't know about her incident. I guess this newspaper stuff is growing on me: making me think too much. Anyway, Pat took her wig off for bed, which gave me a whole bunch of other things to think about. I rubbed her back until we both fell asleep

CHAPTER TWELVE

SONIA

The press conference accomplished its goal though not the way I thought it would. First of all, nothing of interest could happen in a meeting room at a hotel in Fond du Lac. Secondly, the press that attended was there to cover the movie and its star. Thirdly, I really had nothing to say that was of any interest. And fourthly, I just may be over the hill at twenty-three…at least as a celebrity. Mom says I should go back and find my writing and forget all the other stuff. It's going to be hard to just be me again and I find myself embarrassed and angry. The former because I saw yawns in the audience and only one guy even took my picture. The latter because even Des wasn't there. If he was in town he should have been there. He should have found me and at least been concerned about me. If he was in Ireland where he belongs I wouldn't be in this snit, but come on, Desmond!

Okay, I got that out of my system. Yeah, I was jealous as heck when Sarah Dylan took over and the cameras started popping up. Joan said it would be a neat 'double play' since Sarah was playing my mom. I get it that Joan is working for Stompe Publishing and trying to capitalize on everything newsy to sell books. Then I'm thinking, hey, someone took a shot at me in Nairobi. Look, I now have a scar on my cheek. Doesn't everyone want to love me up again like they did when I was kidnapped and held for ransom? Where are all my fans? Cue the world's smallest violin playing something Irish.

So time passes and so does fame. I waded in pity until Mom and I took a walk just before dark. It was one of those lavender-to-purple evenings that remains in afterglow mode until almost ten o'clock. We walked up to The Ledge and through the trees to take in the view.

"Does your jaw hurt from clenching it?" Mom asked me. I was instantly disarmed and smiled.

"Yeah, it hurts. Been clenching it all day...but I'm okay now, Mom."

"Good. I think I know what you are feeling, but since when do you hold it all in like that?"

"I don't know. I guess I am confused about a few things."

"Let me guess. Sarah stole the show. Des didn't show up and Bim was the only person who wanted to interview you."

"You're good."

"I'm your mom. Take a seat."

We had come to a fallen tree which made a natural bench looking out at the view of Lake Winnebago. I saw still water reflecting lights from the far shore. The western sky was cloudless and the dark violet end of the spectrum banded from horizon to zenith. It was breathtakingly quiet until you really listened. Then I heard night birds, probably barn swallows with whispering wings zooming around below us.

"Do you know this spot, honey?" Mom asked.

"Maybe I was here before. I'm not sure."

"This is the place where Roland and Mike sat just before Papa had his stroke. It was winter then. Different kind of view, but still beautiful."

"Mom, sometimes I have a hard time remembering Papa."

"You were pretty young then and we didn't know him for long."

Mom looked out at the darkening lake and nodded her head. I could feel her smile.

"Papa left us more than Ghost Farm and his fortune, you know."

"He left us his love," I whispered.

Mom put her arm around me. "More than his love even. He left us his heritage as a writer, Sony. Everything that has happened to you, the good and the bad, has come because you are a poet first and by choice. You became a celebrity by chance and someone else's choice. Would it be so hard to go back to your writing and get serious about it again? You are so talented and yet you have been distracted by all of the attention."

"It all just happened. What was I supposed to do?" I felt like those words were asking for tears. I tried to hold them off.

"Hey, you did everything right. But, maybe now it is time to take control of your life and apply it to the things you will really be remembered for."

"Sometimes being a poet sounds dumb." I had pondered that too often.

"Hah, in this day and age maybe. People confuse song lyrics for poetry and blog entries for purple passage prose. People need to listen to a clearer voice from time to time and poets provide that. They always have since we crawled out of the caves. Maybe even before then. Your verse is your voice. It is a true gift."

"I don't know…"

"I do. Papa did. And so do those people who discovered you and read your books before your face got famous for the wrong reasons."

"So what do I do next?"

"Why don't you move into my writing studio for a while and crank some work out."

I let the nightfall work that idea over in my head for a minute. The greatest book I had ever read, *The Needle's Eye* was written in that old cheese shed by Roland. Mom had written her best work in that place. To have it handed over to me was an important gift and opportunity. Maybe it was time.

"Let me go look at the shed. It's been a while since I was in there."

"Okay," Mom said and stood up.

We started walking back toward the moon rise above The Ledge. "Can I sleep there tonight?"

"It's all ready for you, Sony."

We walked a little farther. "Mom, there is one more thing…"

"Des?"

"Yikes, you *are* good."

"What's going on with you two?"

"I guess I won't know the answer to that until I see him. But, maybe he never even stopped here? Maybe he was passing through? I never have been able to figure him out."

Mom stopped walking. Even in the dark I could sense a mood swing.

"What, Mom?"

"Honey, I talked to Pat tonight. As you know she has a grapevine like no one else in this town. It seems she knows a realtor who just rented a house to an Irishman who fits Des O'Conner's description and shares his name. "

"He rented a house around here?"

"Not just a house, Sony."

"Huh?"

"He rented that one." I followed Mom's pointing finger to the top of the rise. In the moonlight I could just make out Meg Bollander's place above us. There was indeed a light on in the front window. All I could do was stare until the proper poetic words were formed.

"Holy shit!"

CHAPTER THIRTEEN

DESMOND

I woke up in the chair to the sound of something scurrying across the floor. A mouse was my guess. In a way I found it comforting to have at least one roommate to share all this splendid squalor. If I had adjusted my watch properly it was around three in the morning and still fairly warm. I had opened every window that was not jammed shut in an effort to air out the house. The realtor had told me it had been abandoned for almost ten years. I could believe that. It seems the previous owner had moved away suddenly and left a sort of archeological site for me to sift through. I poured another glass of whiskey and began to explore.

The living room was dominated by a single easy chair that faced the window. I had found an old afghan draped over it that seemed to tell the story of someone who spent many a night where I had just spent my first. The shelves of knick-knacks advertised that I was indeed in Wisconsin—all of them themed in that way. I had been to the bathroom already and found it functional, but filthy with insect corpses and hard water stains in the basin and commode. The tub was the sarcophagus for a dead toad. Lovely.

One of the two bedrooms had a closet not quite full of women's clothes, whose style had disappeared from the earth at least fifty years ago. The bed was made and obviously had not been slept in for ages since it was covered with boxes. Further investigation revealed that the boxes were filled with painting supplies. Some had never been opened. So I'm thinking we have an elderly lady who was an artist. The picture was forming in my mind. The other bedroom smelled of paint and turpentine. Another made bed, but the spread was stained with paint. Nothing in that closet.

Pictures? There were none on either walls or surfaces. No family portraits or even a pet. I deduced she was a spinster. The liquor bottles under the kitchen sink would seem to confirm the loneliness theme I was following. Kitchen cabinets were barely stocked with a few cans and boxes. Nothing edible except to mice who had gnawed into the cereals.

I did find some unopened mail within a stack of old newspapers. The letters were addressed to Meg Bollander. The last name when attached to the first sounded vaguely familiar to me. I would have searched her out on the computer, but there was and, I suspect, never had been any internet access in this place. I made a note to see about that in the morning. There was a lot more exploring to do, but the whiskey was making me sleepy so I went back to the soft chair with the view. Once in a while headlights flickered down on the highway as I guessed folks were early risers in these parts. Most of the traffic was moving south toward the city of Fond du Lac, whose lights filled the view to the extreme left, if you stood and went to the window. One could see a farm down below with a yard light. Another group of lights were off to the right on the highway. The small town of Pipe, I guessed.

I switched off the lamp next to the chair and got comfortable, almost to sleep, when I heard a rapping on the kitchen door. I mistook it for another creature until the rapping got louder and more insistent. I got up and warily made my way in the dark. I found a light switch by the door and flipped it. My first thought was that I was dreaming because Sonia Costello was standing on my porch. The light made her flinch and she backed up a step as I opened the door.

For an odd second or two neither of us said a word. Sometimes when a person occupies such a large place in your imagination the presence of the real live human being seems unreal. The activity that began to fire in my brain was blinding, confusing, overwhelming. And yet, here was this pretty young woman in t-shirt and jeans with her curly dark hair pulled back looking just as I remembered her from the last time I saw her almost a year ago. I wondered what I looked like to her. She spoke first.

"Sorry. Were you asleep?" she whispered.

"No," I said though still not sure. I cleared my throat wishing I had not had that last drink. I was vaguely aware of what I smelled like.

"Well?" she said. Still no smile.

"Um, yes, please come into my castle." My words were as stale as my breath. There would be no kiss anyway, it seemed. Sonia walked past me into the kitchen.

"Wow, this place is a mess."

"Isn't it?"

"How long do you plan on staying here, Des?"

"Well, actually…"

"Why are you staying here is what I really want to know." Definitely no smile yet.

"This is an odd hour for this conversation, don't you think?"

"No, what I think is odd is that you are living in Meg Bollander's house right above Ghost Farm."

"Ghost?"

"Ghost Farm. My family's home." She had walked through to the living room with me trailing behind. She went to the window. "Mom and Owen live right down there."

"I stood beside her and looked down at that yard light. Now I knew why she was here and why there was no smile. My adventure to Wisconsin had been revealed in the worst way to her. Obviously, news traveled fast around here as it does in all small communities. My proximity to her family farm made me a stalker, plain and simple. How to explain all of this? I sat down in the old chair, switched on the light, and finished my Scot's whisky. I was thinking.

"You're drinking at 3:40 in the morning?"

"Poets drink at 3:40 in the morning. The rest of the drunks are asleep by now."

"Very funny, Des."

Sonia stood with her arms folded and legs crossed leaning against the wall by the window. I thought she looked beautiful in the yellow light of the lamp. I was beginning to wake up and come around to explaining myself.

"Okay, listen to me," I began. "I had no idea where this place was in relation to Molly's house. I swear that on my mother's eyes. Okay? As for me being here in the first place, well (here came the lie) I found out about your close call in Nairobi and figured you would come home. I flew here to make sure you were okay. Are you okay, Sonia?"

Ah, a little fudging with time frames and protective concern might just squeak me by. She was thinking about it, but still no sign of a smile.

"Why did you rent a house? How long were you planning on checking on my health? This doesn't make a bit of sense. If I didn't know you and semi-understand how your twisted mind works I'd call the police. This is not normal behavior, you know. You don't call me for almost a year and then you move into this house. Here! Tell me the truth or I swear I'm gonna get you thrown out of town."

Fighting words. American fighting words. Could she have me 'thrown out of town?' I pictured myself being escorted by the local sheriff to the city limits and kicked in the arse. Well, that was enough. This was when the Blarney was supposed to kick in and tables were to be turned. But, just then I had an odd feeling—a presence in the room. It was though a large hand was placed on my shoulder. A hand that demanded the truth. The hair stood up on the back of my neck. Read this and be assured that there was no Blarney in what I spoke next.

"Can you at least sit down?" She deigned to perch on the edge of a coffee table. "I was in Limerick and restless, okay? I used to see your face all the time in those 'people' magazines, but not lately. I felt I had lost my muse. I couldn't write a word. My wife was hanging over my head like the dark cloud that she is; keeping me imprisoned emotionally. The only thing I could think of doing was to come here. I lied. I didn't know about your shooting incident before I came. I didn't think you would be here. I came just to be able to visualize where you had grown up. I did not plan to contact Molly or Owen. I was going to just come here and see what happened to me. It was a dark lark. Sort of like driving past the house of an old lover if only to make oneself sentimental or melancholy. I find those elements essential to poetry. I think I wanted to write something very personal to you and I needed to be close to your source. I…"

"Oh, stop it, Des."

"I am not lying."

"I know that."

"You do?"

"You were looking at me while you talked. You look away when you lie. I saw enough of that before."

I looked at her; we looked at each other. A bird flew into the window startling both of us back to reality.

"Poor thing," said Sonia, meaning the bird.

"Yes," I said meaning all of us.

"What are you drinking?"

"Oh, uh, Jameson."

"Give me one."

"I thought you didn't drink?"

"There's a lot about me you don't know…anymore. Besides, poets drink at this time of day."

I went to the kitchen and rinsed out a jelly jar glass, poured two fingers, and returned to hand it to her.

"A Flintstones glass?"

"All I could find," I said. "What do we drink to?" I was hoping for something meaningful.

Sonia touched her glass to mine and said, "Yabba dabba doo."

CHAPTER FOURTEEN

MOLLY

The heat wave ended last week. In typical Wisconsin fashion we seemed to fast-forward into autumn at the speed of light. I love the change in seasons, but this month it seems everything is changing around here. Sonia is home, living in the old cheese shed and writing every day. Melanie will be coming home next month to settle in and have her baby in our house. Pat Stouffer is doing well with her cancer treatments, although she has days when she won't even pick up the phone to talk to me. Bim fills me in when I see him, but Carrie and Mike are now living over there so I don't feel like I can just drop by like I used to. Des O'Conner has been a quiet neighbor. I think once Sony got used to the idea that he was up there and doing his own writing she rather liked it. I have no idea what is going on between them and really don't want to. Melanie will take a different stance, I fear, when she gets here. She has never liked Des. So who's left? Owen, of course.

Owen is the object of my biggest change. I say object, but he is not doing the changing, I am. Our relationship has evolved from an awkward courtship to a lasting love, but even that requires some sort of shape. We have called it a partnership. I have felt for a while now that that was not enough. In short I want to marry Owen. Sounds simple, but I have struggled to frame the proposition because it is he who has proposed marriage to me on several occasions and I have been the one who turned him down in favor of the status quo. I know it sounds silly that I can't get the right words out of my mouth to the man I share a bed with, but there it is. Writer lacks words.

The film crew that has been around here for the last month and a half has pretty much finished their work. Most of the crew is gone leaving what they call the second unit to redo a scene or two that didn't work the first time. I was telling Owen that I was going to miss the attention that the director gave me and he suggested we throw a wrap party at Ghost Farm for whoever is still around. The more I thought about it, a party might be just the thing to get the planet back in proper orbit. I made the phone calls and it looks like we are having an end of summer bash.

I wanted to run some things about the party past Sonia and I found her in the cheese shed on her cell phone. She waved me in and made a quick goodbye to whomever she was talking to.

"Sorry to disturb you, babe. Got a minute?"

"Sure, what's up?"

Now I could tell she had been talking to Des. Even though my daughter has cocoa brown skin she can still blush with the best of them. I sat down on the arm of the sofa.

"Des?"

"Yeah, we talk, but I am kind of staying away."

"And he is okay with that arrangement?"

"Mom, this so complicated."

"I know."

"But, you don't."

I slid from the arm of the sofa onto a cushion and settled next to my daughter. "I'm all ears." That made her laugh, which was a good start.

"Okay, Mom, he's here right? I mean he is right here in our backyard. He's not in Ireland or Boston. He's living in Meg's house for god's sake."

"What's it like up there…I mean the house?"

"It's a freaking mess. He has not cleaned anything. It is in the same shape it was when Meg moved to California. She even left dirty dishes in the sink. He just sits in her chair in the living room and doesn't do anything about the place."

"And you don't like that?"

"I'm not a messy person." She looked at me and rocked her head back and forth.

"Well, not anymore."

"Go on," I said. Sony was beginning to round the curve and head into her point.

"We are not sleeping together, okay?"

"Is that good or bad, honey?"

"Good. Well, you know…"

I didn't want to know about the details of their relationship. I have an imagination. Sleeping with a separated man is not a sin, but it can be damaging if there is no endgame to the relationship. I could see Sony was in love limbo. I was kind of there myself to a much lesser degree.

"How do you want this to turn out? You know down the road. In the future."

"I see it going nowhere, Mom. When I finish my latest collection I plan on going back to Africa for a while. He will eventually go back to Ireland."

I should mention here that Sonia established a school in Kenya after her kidnapping a few years ago. That school has become her home away from home. She was not welcomed in Sudan by the new government because she represented old wounds. Something stupid like that. I have never understood the politics of that region. Anyway, she does what she can to encourage young girls to get an education and her school specializes in teaching writing skills. It's neat. It works. But, now I am scared to death of her going back to where she was shot at. How can I express that fear when I know she'll go anyway?

"So, his little visit to Wisconsin means nada?" I asked.

"Hmm. Not necessarily nothing, he is sweet to me. He is up there writing poems about me, about being here. He won't let me read them, but I know they are beautiful because that is what he does. That's how he won…"

She cut herself off. Maybe too much information was about to come out.

"Its okay, Sony, I know he is charming." The next part was hard for me to say. "If you two are in love then you are going to have to figure something out. People who are in love want to be close to each other. They need to be together."

"Yeah, I know, like you and Owen."

"We almost didn't make it."

"But, there is no solution, Mom. He will never divorce her."

"Well, there is legal divorce and there is emotional divorce. Can you live with one and coexist with the other?"

"You sound like Des."

"I am trying to sound like you, babe."

The great conversation ender called the cell phone interrupted us. She reached for hers and I reached for mine. Mine won. It was Carrie Gabler wanting to do lunch. I told her I would pick her up at noon. She could help me plan the party. I hung up and looked at Sonia, who had knit her eyebrows in thought.

"Sorry, honey, you want to talk some more?"

"When is this party?"

"Saturday afternoon."

"Can Des come?"

"Why not?"

"Yeah, why not? The press sure doesn't care anymore. right?"

"Well, actually, Sarah and Jon will be there so there might be someone lurking at the end of the driveway."

"Or in our oak tree?'

There at last was the blinding smile I loved. Sonia had just grasped one of life's most useful lessons: our lives are, if nothing else, stupidly humorous. If you take yourself too seriously, you miss the big joke being played on yourself. That joke is always there in the background waiting for the rim shot. Sonia had just heard it.

"Can I go to lunch with you and Carrie?"

"Of course. That would be great."

I left my daughter smiling. Mission accomplished. I felt energized and all the talk about love made me gravitate to Owen. I headed for the yellow barn.

As I mentioned, Owen had moved his veterinary practice from Long Lake to our farm about nine years ago. The move had been more successful than either of us had imagined. Ledge Veterinary Clinic was popular not just because folks liked Owen or the fact that it was nicely located in a crack between towns. It was a happy place, a magical place to bring your pet. We had fixed up the barn to accommodate a modern animal clinic, but most of the charm of the old building was left intact. Clients could walk through the clinic area and pass into the old barn, which we had made into a Roland Heinz museum. In the middle of the original floor were the same three old lawn chairs that Roland and the kids used to sit in and watch the family barn owl watch them.

There were also some very rustic display cases which were antique cabinets of Amish design. In them were manuscript pages and other artifacts of Roland's life. Photographs of Roland, donated by Mike Gabler, hung from the walls along with other bits and pieces of memorabilia that old friends had given us. I always thought it looked like some sort of a cathedral inside that part of the barn partly because of the light. While the roof had been repaired, we turned the original holes in the roof into windows. The light of each day decided the mood in the barn, just as it always had.

Owen was in his office when I came in.

"Hi, honey," he smiled. "Whatcha up to?"

"About 5' 4", I said and sat down across from him. I really wanted to say, hey let's get hitched. The time wasn't right today. He sensed something.

"What's wrong?"

"Why do you say that?"

"You're looking like you're thinking hard about something. You have that look."

"I just had a talk with my youngest." A quick deflection.

"Oh, about…" He moved his head in a way I knew he meant he was nodding towards Meg's old house.

"Bingo."

"Anything new with them?"

"Not according to her."

"So what then?"

"Oh honey, I just feel for them. Yeah, both of them. They have become like characters in their own poetry. Tragic and beautiful all at the same time."

"Do I need to say something here like it's their lives?"

I wanted to scold Owen for reminding me of that fact for the hundredth time, but of course, he was right for the hundredth time.

"Okay, that's it. No more information."

"But, you'll fill me in at bedtime, right?"

"You know me too well."

"I know I love you, Molly."

Okay, there was my opening. It almost came out. "I wanted to ask you something, but I think I'll wait for bedtime for that, too." Gutless.

"Sounds like fun."

"Maybe not what you're thinking. Anyway, the girls are going out for lunch today. Me, Sony, and Carrie. I may be too wiped out for anything later."

"No Pat?"

"She doesn't feel well today. Carrie invited us, probably to take a break herself."

"Have fun. I've got a busy afternoon ahead."

I left the barn feeling like we had unfinished business. Timing is everything.

CHAPTER FIFTEEN

BIM

You know where I am. It's raining cats and dogs out in my driveway, but it's nice and cozy here in the garage. I came out early this morning because the house is too full of people. Having Mike and Carrie home is nice for Pat, but I can't keep up with all the conversation and chit-chat. Mike is on the phone constantly apologizing to someone or other about being here. Carrie, I know, is uncomfortable with her mom's illness and dotes on her too much. I was sitting her wondering which one of them would gravitate to the garage first. I was betting on Mike, but it was Carrie.

"Good morning, Bim. I need a beer."

Well, that declaration coming from a beautiful woman took all the dampness and gloom out of the morning. Carrie is so strikingly beautiful that men either stare into her sun or look away quickly to avoid being blinded. I'm too old to be blinded so I just look at her face in awe. I cracked a cold can of Busch and handed it over. I only had two on ice for the day, but cutting my rations in half for Carrie was just fine.

"You need a break, Carrie?'

"Umm, maybe. Mom is on the phone with Molly and Mike is on the phone with whomever."

"That phone is attached to his ear."

A blinding smile. "You noticed that, huh?"

"Look, it's great that you kids are here for us, but you don't have to sacrifice your own lives to be here. We would both understand if you needed to go home."

"Both of you?"

Okay, she had me. Pat loved having them. It was a distraction if nothing else. And the days after chemo were tough for her, which left me on my own.

"Okay, neither of us. Thanks again for coming, Carrie."

Carrie nodded, but then drifted off. The rain can do that to you; warm mesmerizing splashes making the flower beds wince.

"You went out with Sonia last night, huh?"

"Yeah, you know, we hit a couple places for old time sake."

"Any ghosts?"

I could tell by Carrie's return to focus that I had hit on something.

"Some people never leave this town, do they, Bim? I mean just for laughs we went to the Back Room for a beer and I swear some of those men were still sitting in the same place with the same clothes drinking the same drink. It was like no time had passed at all."

"What were you expecting?"

"I don't know…change."

"Hah, not much changes around here; especially out there in the Holyland. Those old farmers live to be a hundred. Milking cows and shoveling their shit must be some sort of fountain of youth. Did they remember you?"

Now came a wicked smile. "Oh yeah, they remembered me."

The way she said it made me curious. "Like who? Anyone I know?"

She shook her head. "No one you know. I saw a man I used to well…date. He was very nice and friendly, but it brought back a bunch of old memories. You know, my past life. Bim, I ran away from that life a long time ago and thought maybe it had dissolved with time around here."

"But, it's still lurking, eh?"

"Yeah, I mean I was a mess back then. I got around a little too much. You know."

"All that don't mean shit no more and you know it, Carrie. And don't beat yourself up over the damned past."

She stared out at the rain and had a sip of beer.

"You know what's weird, Bim? Why seeing that guy really scared me? Because I like being flirted with again. I had just enough beer in me to flirt back, too. If Sony wasn't with me I don't know what I would have done."

Well, this was getting interesting: Carrie using me as her confessor. Must be something disarming about an old coot in a wheelchair that triggers trust. I saw Mike go by the kitchen window and figured I'd better give her absolution before he came outside.

"Okay, listen girl. We all got a past and it triggers different feelings in different people. Some shut it out completely, some react to an old face or place. Deep down inside you is still that Wisconsin girl, the one who grew up here and followed the local ways. You drank too soon. You smoked too soon. You went off with boys too soon. So what? You think now that you live in Massachusetts that your little badger bitch is gone away?"

I was being stared at now as I suppose I was hitting sore nerves one by one.

"Mike found you and fell in love with that old girl. You must have been doing something right back then. Father Stouffer says say three Hail Marys and call me in the morning. The past is overrated anyway. The neighbor who lives three doors down watches a tape of the Packers Super Bowl game from 1997 every damned day of the week. Let it go for cry-eye. Tell you what, the present sucks right now around here, but I got an eye on the future and things will get rosy again. For all of us."

Carrie aimed those glacier blue eyes at me, stern at first and then they melted into a smile that any man would die for.

"You know who you sound like? Roland Heinz."

"Maybe I picked up a little from him."

"You amaze me, Bim. I mean, how do you sit in the garage 365 days a year and get so wise?"

"It's only about 350 days. The wisdom comes from the beer."

She stood up and kissed me on the top of my head. I felt the thrill down to my toes. "You're the prettiest girl I ever saw, Carrie," I called after her. She sort of did a little hip swing as she headed for the house, never looking back until she got to the door. From there she smiled at me and stuck out her tongue. Little badger bitch!

Mike was my next customer of the day. I always liked this guy, although we had never spent much time together. He is so caught up in his photography work that I could see how Carrie might get distracted by some old beau in a bar. Don't get me wrong, him and her were tight; business partners and married partners, but they had found each other later in life. Sometimes when there are no children to relive your own childhood, things can get dull. I think some of that happened to me and my first wife. No kids led to no love, but there was more to it than that. Anyway, Mike…

"Good morning, Bim. When is this rain going to stop?"

I hear Mike and think of Jack Kennedy. It's the accent. Now, Mike will be the first to tell you that we Wisconsinites have a funny accent, too. I get that because the Holylanders talk even funnier than we townies do.

"Rain'll let up by this aft. What are you up to today?"

"Well, I'm flying out again tonight for a one day shoot in Detroit."

"Detroit? What the hell they got there to photograph?"

"They got a hot rapper."

"Hah, I thought rap went the way of disco."

"You know music?"

"Since I got my own computer I know every damn thing on earth…whether I want to or not."

"How do you like your writing career? Pat sends us clippings even though we can read them on the web."

"It's okay. Helps pass the time. I coulda used you a couple weeks ago when I did a story on Sonia. I'm supposed to take my own pictures, but I never can remember my camera. Anyway, the stroke kind of limits my mobility. You know."

"Maybe I can get some pictures for you this weekend at Molly's party. I heard Sarah Dylan will be there, too."

"You know her, I'm guessing."

"Yeah, we did a couple sessions with her."

"Well, here's another tip for you. That Irishman is here in town. Living up at the old Bollander place. Used to be a lot of pictures of him and Sony in those supermarket rags. Is there any money in that sort of stuff?"

I could see Mike was choosing his words carefully. I kind of knew what he was going to say.

"Well, there used to be more interest in them than there is now. I mean, those things come and go."

"You mean the scandal. Him being married and then putting the moves on her?"

"Bim, nothing is ever exactly what it seems."

"I've noticed."

"I know both Sonia and Desmond. What the paparazzi did to them was a shame. I never sell anything to the supermarket papers."

"You don't have to, right?"

"No, and I get your point. Even dirt sells. Especially dirt Besides, our families are intertwined so ethically I would not exploit Sonia."

"Carrie would kill you."

"Molly would kill me first. Remember I knew her before I met Carrie."

"But, you will bring your camera to that wrap party, right?"

"I always carry a camera."

"Get me a nice shot of Sony. That's all I ask. Maybe with me in it?"

"You got it, Bim."

I was beginning to warm up to the idea of this party. I might even get another column out of it with photos. I still get around.

CHAPTER SIXTEEN

SONIA

I was sitting in a lawn chair just outside the kitchen door sipping a glass of white wine when I spotted Desmond coming down the hill from Meg's house on foot. For some reason he looked so out of place as he headed for our party. The only other person I had ever seen come down that hill was Meg Bollander, but it was more than that. I put myself inside Des' head and tried to see what he was seeing. This wasn't Ireland; it was Wisconsin in September. The large lake that loomed before him was not some deep loch, but rather our shallow sturgeon tub, long and pale blue today. He would be looking down at Ghost Farm and seeing the group of people and he would be rehearsing his lines to be delivered with Irish charm and humor. I also picked up what I perceived as an aura of fear surrounding his handsome head as he entered the backyard.

Besides me, Mom, and Owen, we were entertaining Jon Greenwood and Sarah Dylan. There were also about five other members of the film crew drinking beer like it was water and hovering over the grill like they had never seen a brat before. Well, maybe they hadn't. Pat and Bim were parked at the picnic table under the oak tree looking very happy to be in the country for the day despite the fact we don't have a garage for Bim. Mike and Carrie were in the house talking to Mom, who was chopping salad and Owen was making sure everyone had a drink. No one noticed Des except me…and Sarah.

While I was waiting for him to walk over to where I was sitting she intercepted him and suddenly my day was not so sunny. She slid her arm into his and led him into the group like he was her date at her freaking party. My first thought was where did they know each other from? My second thought was maybe I didn't want to know. My glass of wine went down in one gulp and hit the bottom of my stomach like a chilled anvil. Jealousy was not the emotion I would have predicted for the day, but it had arrived like unexpected lightning.

Des did catch my eye and I thought I saw a 'rescue me' look, but I was frozen to my chair. He danced Sarah over to me. She was still clinging to him like he was a teddy bear she had won at a carnival. My carnival!

"Hello, Sonia, lovely day," Des deadpanned. I was instantly pissed off that he didn't call me Sony like he usually did. Was he being formal because of her? I was doing a fast burn and he knew it. Sarah was being wonderful and oblivious.

"Well, I know you two know each other," she beamed, like it was an old joke. I just stared at Des. We were definitely communicating with our eyes now.

I stood up and broke my silence. "Hi, Des, you want a beer?"

I didn't hear his reply, but rather walked over to the old galvanized washtub filled with beer, wine, and ice. I filled my glass and grabbed two cold ones. I think I must have walked back like I was blindfolded and handed each of them a can. At least Sarah let him go long enough to take the beer. I didn't look at Des and quickly walked away, but only got a few paces before someone grabbed my arm. It was Bim Stouffer.

"Nice day, Sony…except for that storm cloud over your head."

Bim was seated at the table with his walker next to him. Pat had gone over to talk to Owen so we had a moment to ourselves.

"Why do you say that, Bim?"

"Hah, you don't sit in the garage for all those years and not notice things. Sit down for a sec."

When I was a kid I used to think Bim was weird. I figured him for just a beer-drinking coot who just sat in his garage all day. I suppose that was true on the surface, but Bim has a depth to him, too. I had learned to trust him, a gift I did not give away freely.

"Okay, you busted me. I am pissed off."

"Figured. I saw that little drama developing all the way from Meg's house. Looks like the actress and the poet know each other."

"You think?"

"Know each other, but that's about it in my estimation."

"Huh?"

"Body language, Sony. If they were trying to hide something about themselves at your party they wouldn't be any where near each other. Besides, she was the aggressor. Your pal walked right into it and now he doesn't know what the heck to do about it. You should rescue him."

"Over my dead body." I had just finished another glass of wine.

"Oh, okay, no fighting spirit, huh? If you don't want to fight then don't pout. You're ruining the party."

I was stunned. I wanted to turn my white wine anger on Bim, too, but he was smiling at me. He was pushing my buttons. I finally sat down and leaned into him.

"What should I do? I'm half blasted and fully jealous. Does the garage guru know a way out of this?"

"Garage guru? I kinda like that one. "Here's what you do." Bim whispered his advice in my ear. I blushed and nodded.

While I waited to enact the Bimster's plan I got a phone call. Joan had checked out of the hotel and was on her way to the farm with another person. I asked who and she told me it was an FBI agent named Belforte. I got sober real quick. I had been expecting this for days, but why did it have to be today?

By the time they arrived I had already told Mom and Owen that I was going to need some privacy and Owen told me to use the clinic. I thought that was a good idea. Ever since I was little I always associated the yellow barn with my Papa Roland. I believed his spirit still lived there. I wanted his spirit with me for whatever the agent was going to tell me about Nairobi. This was turning into the strangest day.

I shook hands with Agent Beforte and we all sat in the reception room of the animal clinic. Despite having a couple glasses of wine I was nervous as heck.

"How's the cheek, Ms. Costello?" he asked.

Joan and I exchanged glances, but she would be my silent partner today.

"It's okay. Looks like I will have scar is all."

"Hmm, good," he said as he opened his briefcase and shuffled through some papers. He had the case on his lap so I couldn't see the contents, but I was aware that he had information about me and I was dead curious. I allowed him to get organized while I agonized.

"Ms. Costello, as you know, when you travel and are shot at the government takes an interest. In your case, since you are a high profile person, we would want to know who is threatening you and why. The Kenyan government also is very interested in this incident because of your involvement with the school over there. Then there was your involvement with the NGO and your kidnapping a few years ago."

I nodded. He was getting to something.

"Normally, a near miss like yours does not get much attention. Random shots are fired all the time in the area you were visiting that day. We did not think we would turn up much information, but with a little luck we have stumbled upon something."

"What?" I said. It came out hoarsely.

"Photographs taken by a security camera that was positioned behind you that day."

Now I was nervous. I had an idea what was coming.

"Take a look at these pictures."

He handed me a stack of black and white prints. It took me a moment to orient myself to figure out what I was seeing. The first one clearly showed the stage where the singers were performing. Then I located me as seen from behind. I recognized the backs of the people I was with, too.

"Keep going," the agent said. "We blew the images up."

I went through the photos carefully. I knew what I was looking for. "I see it," I said.

"What do you see?"

"I see the man with the rifle to the right of the stage."

In the photo a black man with sunglasses had his head and shoulders visible through the sunroof or a hole cut in the roof of a van. He had a rifle with a scope and it was aimed in my direction. I could not see the smoke from the shot, but I could see some of the crowd looking around in panic, some at the van and some in my direction. In the next picture one woman is pointing at the van. In the next the van is gone behind the stage. In the strangest picture I have ever seen I saw that I had gone to one knee and was holding my cheek. I remembered the burning. Then I remembered that I thought I saw Ali Assan just before the pain.

"Wow! This is spooky," I said. "Sort of like reliving it."

"Yes, we see the shooter and we see him disappear. Not much to go on, but is there anything else you can glean from these pictures? Take your time."

I scanned the pictures, especially the blowups of the stage. I found the man who looked like Ali. He was definitely staring in my direction in one shot and then looking toward maybe the van in another. I still wasn't sure it was him, though. But, then sometimes you just know something.

"This man. Here." I said and Belforte came over and sat next to me. "I think I recognize this guy."

"Who do you think he is?"

"I could be wrong, but my gut instinct tells me this is Ali Assan."

"The man who kidnapped you? Are you sure?"

"Well, according to him, he was the man who released me, but yeah, that man."

"Interesting. We never have been able to figure out who he is. Maybe now that we have his face..."

I could only nod. I had a million thoughts going through my head.

"Do you think he had something to do with the shooting?" I asked.

"Well, if this is him then it is perhaps more than a coincidence that he would be attending a folk singing festival in a Nairobi slum. What do you think?"

"I don't know what to think. Now I am not sure it's even him."

Agent Belforte put the photos back in his case and closed it. "Let me see what I can find out about the man in this photo, okay? Personally, if this is your Ali Assan then maybe we have a lead. If it is just some look alike then we only have the guy in sunglasses with a gun who seems to be aiming at you."

"It's all so weird." I could be less than profound at times.

"I'll get back to you as soon as I can. There are a number of possibilities out there. In the meantime, I suggest you stay away from your school in Kenya for a while until we figure some of this out."

"I plan on staying here through the end of the year."

"Good idea," he said as he stood up. All of us stood.

"Thanks for coming," I said lamely.

"I'll be in touch."

Then poof, he and Joan were gone. When I returned to the party, Des and Sarah were gone, too, along with the plan Bim and I hatched to rescue Des. My head was swimming. I was a little frightened and pissed off again.

CHAPTER SEVENTEEN

DESMOND

I knew I shouldn't have walked back up to my place with Sarah, but she was insistent and I was, well curious. Besides, Sony had disappeared and I was angry and uncomfortable being at Molly's house without her. Well, okay, I assumed Sarah was hitting on me until we got back to my house. Then I wasn't so sure. I had tried to explain to her what a mess the place was, but she practically burst through the door.

"Oh my God," she said as she passed through the kitchen and into the front room. "So this is where she did it!"

I was stunned and confused. "She did what? Who? What are you talking about?"

"You idiot, Des, don't you even know who Meg Bollander is?"

"Um, the lady who used to live here?" That part I did know.

Sarah looked at me like I was crazy. "You really don't know do you?"

I shook my head.

"Meg Bollander is a very important American painter. She now lives in California, but this house is where it all started. I own seven of her paintings."

"But how did…?"

"I was talking to Molly before you came down to the party. I asked her about Meg and she pointed up to this place. Then she told me you were renting it. My God, what a small world we live in."

Sarah prowled around the room and then headed for the other rooms. I didn't know whether to follow her or not. I mean, it seemed like I was not the reason she wanted to come up here. I had been flattering myself falsely into thinking this gorgeous movie star was interested in me, when it turned out she was an art collector and I happened to live in a museum. Life is tricky. I plunked down in the big chair and stared glumly out the window as I listened to closets and cabinets being opened and shut. I knew I had pissed off Sony on an ego lark. I suddenly needed to get back to the party.

"Oh, Sarah," I called. She walked back into the front room, obviously enjoying her snooping.

"This is so cool, Des. Imagine it all started here. You can still smell the paint and thinner."

"Yes, well, I am glad you found your art Mecca, but I think we need to get back before…"

"Before Sonia misses you?"

"Something like that."

"Poor, poor man," she said and placed herself between me and the picture window. To my astonishment she began to undress.

I was dumbstruck and could not speak. I could only watch and wonder how many men on earth had had this fantasy. Her clothes fell into a tiny pile at her feet and then she slinked over and straddled me. She kissed me and yeah, I was aroused.

"I want to do it in Meg Bollander's house," she hissed and began unbuttoning my shirt.

It's funny how a million things can go through your mind in a nano-second. It seemed like I was going to have to take the ultimate test of love. I was going to be asked to betray every male hormone in my body for a romantic dream I had been tossing about for years. Could any impossible love compete with what was on my table or my lap right now? In one more moment it would be too late.

I will confess, as I must, that I came very close to not pushing Sarah Dylan onto the rug. But, I did.

"Maybe you should be trying to fuck Meg Bollander!"

I will never forget the look on her face. It was a close-up from one of her films. She did not need to act, however. She was amazed and shocked…and then she burst into laughter. As she laughed she actually tried to modestly cover herself with her arms.

"Shit, I sure wish I could find a man like you, Desmond O'Conner. You really are the poet, aren't you?"

I knew, of course, what she meant. Sony. Without being able to prove it I had just told Sony I was finally and deeply committed to her. It felt very good and very bad at the same time. I was being mocked, right?

"You are free to rummage around here, if you wish, but I'd better get back down there."

The little actress made some expressions of undefined mirth, rage, whatever and then waved me off. Dismissed, I was from me own house. It was a long walk back down to Molly's. Sonia was sitting in a sulk so I knew she had seen me coming.

"Let's go," I said and took her arm. She resisted. People were now staring at us.

"You bastard!" she half-whispered, half spat.

"Almost, but not quite. Do you have a car?"

Sonia turned from me to look at the old gentleman standing with a walker. I saw him nod to her.

"Yeah, I have a car. Where are we going?"

"I don't know. For a ride. Someplace else."

Sony stood and we walked to the driveway as everyone went back to their conversations and food. As we drove out onto the highway and turned right I looked off to my right and saw the figure of a woman walking downhill from the art museum that now sheltered an Irish poet. I looked at Sony driving, eyes on the road and hoped I was finally where I was supposed to be today.

"So this is the Holyland, eh? Why do they call it that, Sony?"

She had calmed down to the point that I noticed her knuckles were no longer white from gripping the steering wheel so tight. We had driven off the main highway and were now heading down a country road away from the big lake. Neatly kept farmhouses and fresh-painted red barns popped up every mile or so and Holstein cattle dominated the rest of the landscape. I saw a church steeple in the distance, which had prompted my question. I knew the local name for this area, but not the how or why. I hoped it would be a neutral ice-breaker.

Still without looking at me once, she began. "I always thought it was because most of the towns are named for saints. And also, the Amish people live out here. The towns all have a central church and of course, a tavern nearby. Those are sacred too, around here."

"Ah, hah. And the Amish are exactly what?"

"Mennonites. German or Swiss. They came to Wisconsin with the rest of the Germans because this part of the state looks so much like northern Germany. At least that is what I was told."

"Oh yes, I think we even have some Amish in Ireland. Plain clothing and black horse drawn carriages, right? Beards and bonnets."

"Yeah, I like the way they look. I wrote something about them once."

"Do you recall it, Sony?"

Now she looked at me briefly. I felt a mild thaw. She then recited:

> *Who is that up on the wagon*
> *Black-dressed bearded man I see*
> *Following an energetic mare*
> *From the Holyland to Galilee*
> *From the shore of Winnebago*
> *To the stony beach of Michigan*
> *Who is that ageless driver*
> *Whose hourglass has no sand*

"Lovely, girl...as usual," I said. I had slipped into me deep Gaelic accent, an instinctual reflex to her poetry. "You know there are many other Holylands. My Ireland, your Darfur. Then there are the Holy Lands, the bloody ones poorly named..." My discourse was cut short by a frown that eclipsed the sun.

"Des, what happened this afternoon? And don't tell me a lie because you know I see through those."

"Honesty can be poorly interpreted."

"Save the blarney for someone else."

"Sorry, dear, it was only a preamble to the truth of the matter."

Sony pulled over on the side of the road across from a beautiful Catholic church. 'St. John's Church' it said etched in stone. I wondered if it was a coincidence that my tale was to be told with that stone steeple looming above me. I had no intention of lying anyway.

"She wanted to see the Bollander house. She owns several paintings by the woman who once lived there."

Sony digested that bit slowly. "So it was merely an art appreciation fieldtrip?"

Moment of truth. "It was until Sarah took her clothes off in the parlor."

A loud moment of silence.

"Go on," Sony finally urged. Her brown eyes were x-raying me pretty good.

"She sat on me lap." So Irishly spoken. "She kissed me cold lips. Then I pushed her on the rug before..."

"You pushed her on the rug? Did you follow her down on the rug?"

"I did not."

I could almost feel the roentgens flowing into me. My soul was being scanned. Then, mercifully, she burst out laughing, spitting bubbles of happy mist through her tightly closed and pursed lips.

"You shoved a naked Sarah Dylan onto the rug? She was sitting naked on your lap? Jaysus, Desmond, you are a fool, aren't you?"

"A fool in love with you Sonia Costello."

I got one last deep examination, which I seemed to pass. Maybe.

"Get out," she said.

"Huh?"

"Get out. There's a bar across the street back there and I need a drink. I am assuming that you do, too. You've had quite a day."

Relieved. "That I have."

"Well, wait until you hear about mine."

Outside the car, I had a beautiful woman slip her arm in mine for the second time that day. This time, I believe it was the correct arm.

CHAPTER EIGHTEEN

MOLLY

The end of the party seemed to also be tied into the end of an eventful summer. I was a bit annoyed when Sonia and Des left so abruptly, but I knew I would get the whole story later. In the meantime, there was only me, Owen, Carrie, and Mike left at the kitchen table. The dishes were done and the coffee was poured. Carrie was slicing a carrot cake that she had brought over. I finally let myself relax as Owen did a one-hand massage of my shoulders.

"So who was the guy with Joan?" Carrie asked. She shared her mom's trait of cutting to the chase.'

"Would you believe FBI?" I said, which made Mike's eyebrows go up. Owen already knew.

"No shit, hey?" said Carrie. Her Wisconsin accent had returned very quickly even though I had noticed she had picked up some of Mike's New Englandese. Interesting combination. "What's going on?"

"Well, you guys knew about her adventure in Kenya, right?"

"Who doesn't?" said Mike. "I saw the scar."

"It won't show much," Owen added. He knew a thing or two about scars.

"I only got to talk to her for a minute or two, but Sony said the agent showed her some pictures taken by a security camera the day she was shot at. She said she could see the guy who had the gun, but he was pretty generic, a black guy with shades in a van."

"Wow, then it was no random shot?" said Mike.

"Apparently not. I've got to tell you it creeps me out," I said. It was an understatement. Actually, I was borderline terrified that someone was stalking and targeting my daughter. Maybe even here in Pipe, Wisconsin.

"Well, she's probably safe here, huh?" said Carrie hopefully. I rolled my eyes.

From Mike: "What does this agent think the motive is?"

"Don't know but, I think it still has to do with the kidnapping. There has always been something just not right about how that went down," I said into my coffee cup. "There was money exchanged, but nobody knows by whom and who got it."

"Follow the money." said Owen.

I usually love mysteries. I hated this one. "If we knew who paid the kidnappers we might find out why someone wants Sony…well, you know." Everyone reached for a cake fork at the same time. It was a reflex: feed the anxiety.

"So, she just took off with Desmond, huh?" Carrie asked in an attempt to change the subject. "What's up with them?"

"Owen and I have been asking the same question."

"You know, when you watch them, they do seem to be in love," said Mike.

We now had a subject that I knew plenty about. "Oh, they would be the perfect couple if he was younger, single, and not half-crazy."

Carrie inched her chair a couple inches closer to the table resulting in a floor screech. It added emphasis. "But, Molly, you know as well as I do that none of that matters. It's all window dressing for a moral society. If they are truly in love neither heaven or earth will stand between them."

I nodded. Carrie knew this subject, too. She and Mike were one of those rare couples that had defied odds. They had gone overboard from their two ships passing in the night and met in the water. I kept looking out the kitchen door hoping to see the headlights of a car. I wanted to see Sony before I went to bed. Owen read my mind.

"I don't think they're coming back tonight, babe."

"I suppose," I sighed.

Owen purposely switched channels. "How are things going with Pat and Bim? I talked to them today and they act like everything is fine."

"Well, Mom has her good and bad days. Today was good, which I didn't think it would be after a treatment this week. Bim is Bim, but I worry about him, too."

I put my elbows on the table and leaned in. "This gathering of our families, however motivated, is happening for a reason. Why is everyone home or coming home now? I think it's because we are all going to need to be strong. Pat, Bim, Sony, and soon Melanie and Ray are going through transitions and our little corner of the world is the axle of the wheel."

Everyone nodded. Owen spoke up. "I think its Roland."

All heads and eyes turned to our Dr. Palmer.

"I saw him again last night...in the barn."

"You saw Roland?" Mike asked with a leery smile.

"Oh yeah," said Owen. He looked to me for verification.

"They don't call this place Ghost Farm for nothing," I said.

"He haunts this place?" asked Carrie. I noticed she looked now like a little girl around a campfire. Heck, we all did.

"I saw him the first time years ago, before Owen and I got together. I thought it was a dream, but everything he said came true. Then when Owen moved in we both saw certain things, but didn't compare notes for a while."

"What things?" asked Mike and Carrie simultaneously.

"Well, first it was, like I said, dream-like visitations. A glowing silhouette of a man," I said.

"Then we noticed things being moved around," Owen added. "Mostly books; his books. Then I saw him and that girl out in the barn sitting in those lawn chairs. I could smell blackberry brandy."

"Wait a minute," Carrie injected. "What girl?" Her gorgeous blue eyes were now the size of saucers.

"Garnet Granger," I whispered. Everyone was silent for the count of one, two...

"This is a joke, right?" Carrie asked. Another long silence.

"No joke, Carrie. Too much evidence," I said. "Roland and Garnet seem to live here, too."

"You smelled blackberry brandy?" Mike was looking at Owen. Owen nodded. "You got any? I think I need one."

Owen got up and got a frozen bottle out of the freezer and set four shot glasses on the table. He filled them to the point of surface tension and then lifted his. A toast: "Here's to our families...in all their states of being."

I tossed mine back with the others with one eye still looking for Sonia's car.

Later, I gave up waiting for my daughter and joined Owen in the bedroom. He was already asleep with a book on his chest and his reading glasses still on his nose. I gently put both aside and placed myself next to him. The night was cool and breezy and the old lace curtains danced in a dream-inducing rhythm. It had been a long day and I was asleep before I could rehash it.

I woke up to a noise sometime later and looked at the clock. It was 4:44 AM. Owen was snoring softly. I tried to deny that I had to pee and go back to sleep, but it was impossible so I slipped out and went across the hall to the bathroom. I tripped off all the predictable squeaks in the floor on the way and realized that it was one of those squeaks that had awakened me. Maybe Sony was home?

I took a peek out the bathroom window, but didn't see her car. I didn't think she would have come into the house anyway since she was living in the studio. The girls' old bedroom was fixed up for Mel and Ray. I closed my eyes and relieved myself. When I opened them there was a faint purple glow emanating from the bathtub. I rubbed my eyes and it was still there. I figured all the ghost talk and brandy was making me see things. Or maybe I was still asleep in my bed? Or, just maybe it was Roland!

Sorry to disturb you, dear."
The voice sounded like the flutter of elm leaves. "Roland?"

He ain't here tonight, Molly-a. He said it was time for a little girl talk.
"Garnet?"
Yes, it's me. Sorry. I know you were hoping for him, but I got stuck in your tub and...

"Stuck?"

I was checking it out and so. I like the old ones with the feet and the rubber stopper on a chain. We had one like this when I lived over by Algoma Street in town.

"I remember."

You do?

"It was in 'The Tap Root.' You got stuck in the tub.

And here I am again.

"Why are you here?"

Hah! Well, Roland is in town with his buddy tonight. Sometimes we go a'haunting separately.

"This is nuts"

"Hain'it?

I shook my head trying to clear it. I was still parked on the throne, which made this 'conversation' even weirder than it was. But, I somehow relaxed into it. The young woman stuck in my tub would not disappear.

"So, what sort of girl talk, um Garnet?" The shape changed color to soft gold.

I live in a book and you live in the world. I hear they ain't much different. At least that's what Roland tells me. Right now you have a mystery in your life. You're worried about your youngest. Roland knew she was going to be a writer and he loves her poetry, although I don't understand a word of it. Anyway, the answer to your mystery is very close.

"What are you talking about?"

I know who paid the ransom and why someone tried to shoot her.

"Who…what? I was getting too excited. The tub light was fading. I felt myself floating back to the bedroom. I braced myself in the frame of the bathroom door and looked over my shoulder. "Garnet!"

Look for the messenger bird, Molly-a.

I opened my eyes and looked at the clock. It was 4:58 AM and I no longer had to pee. Owen was snoring softly next to me, but I noticed the old lace curtain hung dead still in the window. Even if it was all a dream suggested by our earlier kitchen conversation, this thing had happened before and I was both excited and scared at the same time. I shook Owen and he woke up with a start.

"What's wrong, honey?" he whispered.

"I want to get married."

CHAPTER NINETEEN

BIM

One bad thing about living a few blocks from the hospital is the sirens blaring away at all time of the day and night. Since it is after 4AM there is no need to make that noise, but those guys from the little towns like to wake us up when they roar in no matter what the hour. Well, I was awake anyway. I try real hard not to take in any liquids after supper so I don't have to get up, but I snuck a couple extra beers at Molly's party so now I pay. Between the siren and the shuffling of me and my walker, Pat woke up. Darn!

"What time is it, honey?" she asked.

"After four."

"Everything okay?"

I could make out her silhouette by the light from a street lamp as she lay facing up. A totally black bedroom would be dangerous for two people who often needed to navigate during the night. Me with my walker and Pat with her plastic waste basket that she used to puke in. What a pair.

"Everything is fine, love. Go back to sleep, okay?"

I crawled back in and we lay side by side listening to each other breathe, I suppose. I had a feeling Pat wanted to talk.

"What's it like for you, Bim?"

"Huh?"

"Tell me what you feel. You know, how did the stroke make you feel. What do you deal with every day? Are you scared?"

I was a little thrown by this kind of talk in the dark. Besides, Carrie and Mike's room was just on the other side of the wall. I turned my head to Pat and whispered.

"Well, I guess I am adapting to this stuff, but some days are rough."

"Tell me."

"Well, just getting around. I gotta plan every move I make. The legs sort of work, but they are stiffer than they ever were before. And this left arm is just sort of a prop."

"You didn't want to do the physical therapy."

"Yeah, I know. I just don't like people touching me. Never did. Except for you."

"What about your mind? That seems like it works okay."

"It works. Maybe too good."

"Why do you say that?"

"Cuz I gotta think about the damage all day. And then what comes next."

"I don't like 'next' either."

"I keep thinking it is going to happen again. I feel like a time bomb. Funny thing is I worry more about making a mess for you than worrying about me."

"I know, me, too."

"So how is for you, Patsy? I see you being sick after your treatments, but you don't tell me about what's going on inside."

"Oh, well, the cancer never did hurt too much. It was more of a presence than a pain. The post-op was painful, but you know, you are so glad when the tumor is removed that it is a nice pain if you can get that. The sickness after the treatments is a lot like a hangover. The worst hangover you ever had. You know when it is coming and you try to prepare, but..."

"It sucks."

"Yep."

"And how is your head, honey? You sure seem tough enough to beat this."

There was a long pause and I thought I was going to hear something I didn't want to hear. Pat always surprises me.

"Look at us, Bim. Layin' side by side in the middle of the night comparing our notes on how we feel. You know how I really feel? Lucky, that's how. At this minute in my life I am exactly where I want to be. I'm in bed with my husband. My daughter and son-in-law are right next door. I am so alive that I can puke one minute and laugh the next. I have good friends who love me and never let me get too down. I got a great grandchild on its way. I can still eat fried fish and have an Old Fashioned on Fridays.

"After mass."

"After mass." She soft punched me in my left shoulder, which was pretty much numb anyway. We both chuckled.

"Most of all," she went on, "I have you, Bimster. You came along at just the right time for me. Whatever 'next' is I don't care as long as we face it together."

Picture a kiss between two people who are completely blind to the wreckage sustained by their elderly bodies. Picture hands, parchment spotted with age, holding on to each other for dear life. Picture the love. Then picture a soft violet glow in the corner of the bedroom over by the cedar chest. That figured. I saw it; I've seen it before. I know it is a winter light, although it can come as late summer turns into early fall in Wisconsin. Roland had come to tuck us back in 'til dawn.

CHAPTER TWENTY

DESMOND

Sonia and I had been too long in that pub in Johnsburg. We had had just enough drink and just enough talk so that we had somehow time-traveled back to our first time as lovers. Well, I suppose it was bound to happen, what with finding a motel and such, but although we slept in each other's arms, we did not make love. I think we both felt the invisible presence of my nameless wife in the room, a spirit so full of spite that she caused us to out-drink our lust. Sony was hard asleep at sunrise, but I was wide awake. I wandered outside the room to look around. The fact was, I couldn't remember much about the place or how we got here.

The inn was called Lake Vista Motel, which indeed it was. Behind the one story building with sixteen rooms flanking an office was the great expanse of Lake Winnebago. Somewhere in our conversation last night, Sonia had told me how Meg Bollander had painted the lake from my living room and had later become famous for her works. She also told me the story of how Meg and Roland Heinz had had a history that included a love triangle ending in hatred on Meg's part. It seems a drama had once taken place in my dirty little rental house. The connection to Roland Heinz, however, is what intrigued me. Now I really wanted to get back and absorb the latent creativity in the house. And Sony always made me want to write: about her and in competition with her. Yes, it's confusing.

So, here I am standing behind a motel in the middle of the USA. My love is in my bed and it is a fine morning, indeed. So, Jaysus, what is wrong with all this? I told you about the first time I met Sony but I didn't tell the whole story. Since it is turning over and over in my mind this morning I think I will try to go over it again…for all of us.

Harry Stompe told me later that his party in Boston way back then was primarily to reconnect me with Molly. Meeting Sonia was supposed to be a little side note in the margins. She ended up being the whole text.

I have spent a lot of time wondering about first attractions. Some people just have a look or an aura, or a vibe that is irresistible. You find you cannot take your eyes off of them. You are delighted and mystified all at once. That was how I was regarding Sony when Molly busted me that first time.

Despite the subtle warning from her mom, I had to approach Sony. After all we were poets published by the same company. I cornered her at the cold shrimp and champagne table and flirted my way into a lunch the next day. Yes, she had spotted my wedding ring very quickly, but I assured her it was all about poetry. I was half right.

In truth, Sonia Costello, was like the final piece of a thousand piece jig-saw puzzle that slid into place completing the picture. This particular puzzle was abstract and wildly interesting. Eroticism mixed with child-like love. I quickly noticed the way her large brown eyes would lock onto mine and how the tiny muscles would cause them to dance precisely with my own eyes. It was mesmerizing. I knew she had no idea she was doing this which made it all the more endearing. I spoke of her having a light around her. It was definitely there, but again, only I could see it and I cherished my secret prize.

Physically, I am tall. She is short. I am as white as marble and she is soft nut brown. I, alas, have been around this planet for many more years than she. I am married and she is free. At first we shared only poetry. I won't share much of my poems here because, well, you can buy them. But, here is one of the first I wrote to her. I assumed much and projected even more;

Cosmic arrow random shot
Arcs across the parking lot
Where spaceships rest
And kids are blessed
With holly

I got home too late
Missed the time and date
Not by light years
But by night tears
Our folly

A simple basic fact
Is that actors always act
Parts badly written
By a hand in mitten
In winter

I can feel your breath
On my face at death
But, not before
An arrow on the floor
In splinters

Well, I guess this poem called *Near Miss* is perhaps too revealing, but I am telling you about Sony and you need to know that I did understand the gulf between us. We closed that chasm maybe too quickly. Then it opened up again. Last night it closed a little. I get dizzy think about what's going to happen next. I fear it will be nothing.

I went back into the motel room and got back into bed with my clothes on. I had been wanting to kiss the scar on her right cheek since I first saw it and now I did. Her brown eyes dawned behind the kiss.

"What are you doing?" she murmured.

"Blessing your wound."

"I don't want you to notice it so much."

"I notice everything about you and I find even your flaws endearing to me. Maybe especially your flaws."

This prompted her to prop herself up on her elbow. "What other flaws?"

"Your flaw of youth for one."

"We've been over and over that, Des. You know that the age thing has nothing to do with us."

Which brought my wife front and center back into room 8 at the Lake Vista Motel. I had cheated on my wife before I met Sony. All of that is meaningless to me, but still indicts me in certain circles. The fact is Sonia and I have only made love once and I have never betrayed her. Oh yes, the tabloids could produce pictures of us together in various places; coming and going from restaurants in New York and Paris. They could show the world how we shared a beach blanket in Miami. They could record a moment of hand-holding in Limerick, but on my mothers' heart, we only made love once. If that seems unbelievable and rather sad, then it is also very poetic…and that is what our souls are made of.

It happened not in a hotel or a house, but in a field. It did not happen on a lovely spring day, but on a cold winter night under the stars. We were stone cold sober and never said a word. It was so spontaneous that there was not even a blanket beneath us. It was everything I ever dreamed about: a coupling that had never quite ended for me. That is why I came here to Wisconsin. I am trying to find the moment again. It didn't happen last night, but I am hopeful. I am Irish, as you know.

CHAPTER TWENTY-ONE

SONIA

I had always been fascinated by the Lake Vista Motel near Quinney. Somehow it always seemed romantic to me. It was so unexpectedly charming; sitting in the middle of nowhere with a spectacular view of Lake Winnebago. It was the first place that popped into my head when Des suggested we find a place for the night. I had already told him, after a brief history of Meg's place, that I would not go back there to sleep. Besides, I wanted to escape from the family for a night. I did not want to have to explain anything to anyone. I had not told Des about the FBI's visit. We were just roaming poets yesterday and that was all I wanted. At the motel we slept together like children too tired to do anything but sleep. When I awoke he was gone, although I knew not far.

I took the opportunity to call Joan. She was back in her office at Stompe even though it was a Sunday. We rehashed the agent's visit for a few minutes and then she said she had another call and would get back to me. I went to the bathroom and looked out the window and saw Des staring out at the lake. Again, I tried to imagine what he was thinking, feeling today. He and I were going nowhere for all the same reasons. The only thing that had changed was the date and location of our conundrum.

My cell phone rang again and it was Joan calling back. I could tell by her voice that something had come up. She informed me that the other call was from Delforte and that he was faxing Joan a picture that she was to forward to me. I waited while the fax came in to Joan. A moment later, Joan told me the new photo was something I needed to see. Of course this perked my interest. I gave her the number for the fax machine in the writing studio. I would check it out and call her when I got home. Then I heard Des fumbling with the key and I dove back under the covers. I don't know why, but I was going to fake being still asleep to see what he was going to do.

I felt the bed rock as he got back in and then I felt him kiss my cheek. The scar. He was kissing my scar. He had gone two weeks without even mentioning it and now he was kissing it. Now, this sounds weird, but I really liked that kiss. I opened my eyes and smiled at him. If he had kissed my cheek once more I think we would have made love. I asked him what he was doing. He said he was blessing me, which was sweet, but I ruined the whole moment by telling him he shouldn't do that. Somehow that led to something about our age difference and then his wife. Now we were just two bad kids in bed in a cheesy motel room. Time to go home.

"So what are your plans, Des?" I asked as we drove south on Hwy 151. He just glanced at me with narrowed eyes. "You don't have one, do you?"

He stared at the road now; I knew he was thinking of something cute to say.

"My plans? Jaysus, what a question for this hour of the day."

"I was right."

"You were right only in the sense that I have not calculated anything beyond the writing I am doing. Oh, and the promotional work I am doing around here."

This last bit threw me. "What promotional work."

"My people at Stompe have set up some book signings here in this area. It seems there is still a small grain of interest in me poetry books."

"Where?"

"Someplace called Appleton. And Kenosha. And Madison," he recited.

"Huh" was my only response. How could he get these gigs for books that had been moved to the bargain tables months ago. Then the lighbulb came on. "This is all timed in to my incident in Kenya, right? It's more a you and me thing than your books. Do 'your people' at Stompe think you can exploit me? Us?"

"Who cares what goes on in their greedy minds? There is no such thing as bad publicity."

I had to think about this. "Well, based on my dud of a press conference here, there is very little interest in me, let alone you, us, we, whatever. Heck, Des, my book sales are flat and have been for a while. Yours must be dead. Sorry." I felt bad about saying that, but it was a reality we both needed to face.

"All those tabloid days and the endless publicity went away two years ago," I went on. You and I, my friend, are not likely to have a boost in sales again until we are posthumous."

"Ah, the Dead Poet's Society is it?"

"Reality, Des."

"How, pray tell me, did we arrive at our gravesites on this beautiful morning?"

I gripped the wheel tightly and shook my head. "Maybe because that is our only future." I started to cry the way some humans do when they find themselves in a corner surrounded by fresh paint.

"Oh Jaysus Christ, Sony, don't start that. If we are washed up as poets then we can always teach the bloody stuff at some damned university."

"No, I mean you and me. We might as well be dead."

I felt his exasperation. He had crying women driving a car that he was trapped in.

"She won't divorce me. We either live in sin or part company? Is that what you want?"

"I don't know what I want!" I semi-screamed. "But, no more motels, okay?"

"T'was your idea."

"And no more Irish bullshit!"

"Okay, stop and let me out! Stop the fucking car!"

I did. I pulled over in Calumetville in the parking lot of a bar. Des opened the door and slammed it when he got out. I drove off with a little squeal of rubber, but slowed down to pull back on the road. In the rearview mirror I saw him looking around. The pub or the highway? I immediately wanted to go back and pick him up. I wanted to make up, but I knew it was useless. It would only lead to more of what had just happened. Anyway, he had a cell phone and money and he was only a couple miles from his house. He'd be fine. I was not that sure about myself.

When I got back to Ghost Farm, I immediately sought the sanctuary of the cheese shed. It looked like Mom and Owen were out anyway as his truck was missing. Maybe they went to church or something. I fell onto the couch with the intention of a long morning sleep, but then I remembered the fax machine. I opened an eye and saw that it had spit a couple of sheets on the floor. There could be no sleep until I looked at whatever Joan had deemed to be so important. What I found I couldn't believe and I knew the idea of a nap was shot to hell.

Fax sheet number one was a cover sheet. Fax sheet number two was a cleaned up close up of the guy I had ID'd as Ali Assan in the crowd at the shooting site. It was fax sheet number three that sent me into orbit. I could scarcely believe what I was holding in my hand. It was a crisp black and white photo of two men smiling wildly into the camera. The location was obviously a pub and a Gaelic verse on a beam behind them ID'd the location as somewhere in Ireland. The man on the right was none other than the man I knew as Ali Assan, only now he was a bit younger with short curtly hair and wearing a cardigan sweater. The man next to him was also smiling a goofy smile and his face was unmistakable. It was Desmond O'Conner. Their arms were around each other!

I studied the picture over and over again making sure my eyes were not tricking me. I was sure now I recognized the pub as Des' favorite watering hole in Dublin. I had been there with him in our heyday. This photo, judging from the men's more youthful faces, was at least ten years old. Probably more. My brain was beginning to short circuit. My first reaction was to go hunt down Des and confront him. Then a weirder idea entered my head. If these men were connected, then

Des might have had something to do with my kidnapping. Or even worse, my shooting. I quickly called Joan back and she told me that Agent Delforte wanted to talk to me ASAP. My hands were shaking as I punched in his numbers.

CHAPTER TWENTY-TWO

MOLLY

After my middle of the night marriage proposal, Owen and I had talked in bed for most of the rest of the early morning. Then we made love instead of breakfast. Later we headed out into the countryside in Owen's truck. I knew exactly where I wanted to go. The kame. It was mostly symbolic, but I wanted his official answer to be given there. We had even joked about getting married on the kame at some point. Today was to be just a little walk out into our past on the way to our future.

Owen had already asked the why-now question early. In fact it was the first thing out of his mouth. I told him about my dream about the girl in the bathtub and he had laughed:

"It took a dream like that to make you want to marry me?"

"Honey, it was a vintage Ghost Farm dream. A visitation. Why would she come to me? I distinctly remember her telling me to 'look for a bird.' It was just like when Roland told me to find the kame."

He was waiting for the upshot.

"The bird must be the owl. The bird that brought us together."

"What else did she say?"

"Something about Sony, I think. I don't remember all of it."

"Well, I don't want to have you marry me under a false premise." I could tell by the tone of his voice that he was humoring me. That alone almost cancelled the deal.

Now it was several hours later, the sun was out and we were atop the glacial kame in the middle of Jersey Flats over in the Kettle Moraine. I have to admit the place did not seem to be as magical as I had remembered it. It was still a pretty and unusual place, but maybe too much time had passed. We both sat down hip to hip on a boulder.

"What are you thinking, babe?" Owen asked.

"I am thinking that maybe I am way too romantic. Too susceptible to dreams. Maybe I want to see ghosts so I see them. Sometimes I wonder if I am delusional."

"Are you having second thoughts?"

"Oh, God, no. It's just that well, Sony and Des got me thinking again."

"I see."

He didn't exactly, but right on cue my cell phone rang it was Sony. I could tell by her tone that something was wrong and Owen picked up the vibe from me. I promised her we would come home right away.

"What was that all about?" Owen asked.

"I'm not quite sure, but something has her upset."

"Des?"

"That would be my guess. Let's go.

We started down the kame and headed for the truck. I quickly realized I had forgotten something: my mission. I took Owen's hand in mine.

"By the way, you were supposed to accept my proposal up there."

"Oh, well how about right here?" He stopped in the meadow which was filled with cornflowers and oxeye daisies. "Yes, I will marry you, Molly Costello. Any time, any place you say."

We continued walking. "How about next month after Mel and Ray get here?"

"Like I said…"

"Good."

And so, about ten years down the road and at the bottom of the Jersey Flats kame, I became engaged to the love of my life. It felt just right. Now we had to find out if our good news was good enough to trump whatever bad news my daughter had. Life is so tricky.

Sonia met us in the driveway, arms folded and frowning. When we got out of the truck she turned without saying a word and led us into the writing studio. Once inside she handed me a copy of a photo and I studied it with Owen looking over my shoulder. He was the first to react.

"It's Des, right?"

I could see it now, too. One of the guys in the picture was Desmond O'Conner.

"What does this mean, honey? Who is the other guy?"

"Mom, I have been studying that picture all morning to make sure my eyes are not messing with me. The other guy is Ali Assan!"

I glanced up from the picture. I could see Sony was sure so I wasn't going to question it. "They know each other? Oh shit!"

Owen took the sheet from my hand and looked it over closely.

"It's definitely Des. Obviously they know each other. Des has his arm around this dude."

"I know," said Sony, "what do I do now?"

That question hung in the atmosphere for a moment while my blood turned to ice water. After all, Des was living right up the hill from us. I wondered now if he was dangerous. I looked to Owen.

"Okay, let's take a step back from panic, ladies," he said. "This photo was obviously taken some time ago, in Ireland, I am guessing."

Sony nodded. I could see the panic in her eyes now, too.

"I think we should confront him and give him a chance to explain."

A light bulb came on in my head. "What about the FBI?"

"Joan said the agent is waiting to hear from me," said Sony.

Owen continued: "Yeah, well evidence-wise this doesn't mean a thing. It links these guys, but…"

"Wait a minute," Sony cut in. "One guy is a Sudanese bandit and the other guy is…my, well you know. What possible link can there be besides some sort of conspiracy?"

"Only Des can answer that question, babe," Owen said trying to sound soothing. He had two crazed women on his hands. "We can't go up there with torches and pitchforks. You want me to go talk to him?"

"Let's all go," I said.

Sony, thought that over, but rejected it. "Owen, I want you to do this for me, okay. I don't trust myself and Mom. We're too pissed off."

"Is he home?" Owen asked.

"He should be by now," said Sony.

Owen took the photocopy and headed for the door. We watched as his truck left the driveway and began the circle around to Meg's old house. Our waiting game had begun. I went in and made coffee. Sonia talked on the phone to Joan. She joined me in the kitchen, where we were both more comfortable and composed.

"This is nuts, Mom."

"I know. That fucking Irishman," I said and for some reason Sony smiled.

"You can write a book about this."

"Crime drama is not my genre, babe."

"Maybe the biggest crime is me falling for him. Whatever he was up to, I let him in willingly."

"Don't start the regrets yet."

"Yeah, but I can't wait for Owen to get back. I want to know how big a fool I have been."

"Listen honey, you don't have to tell me, but what went on with you two yesterday? That was quite a little departure scene you guys did. Sarah and Jon left right after you did and she looked a little too smug. Jon was pissed at her; I could tell that."

Sony smiled again. "Des said he spurned her. She came on to him and…"

"And what?"

"Shit, Mom, maybe he was lying about that, too."

I took a peek through the kitchen windows at the house on The Ledge above us. I would have loved to be a fly on the wall up there.

CHAPTER TWENTY-TWO

DESMOND

I heard the crunch of tires on gravel in the driveway and looked out expecting to see Sony's car. Instead I saw a white pickup truck with a veterinary bed liner and a veterinary caduceus on the door. Dr. Palmer was paying me a house call. I wondered why and as I opened the door for him, I saw by his grim expression that this was no social call.

"Can I come in?" he said.

"Of course, Owen."

He entered the kitchen and looked around at the mess. He shook his head in what I guessed was disgust.

"Come into the parlor, it's a little cleaner," I said. I followed him in and then he turned to face me.

"Who are you, anyway?" he asked.

Well, about a dozen smart answers popped into my head, but I could see by his look that he was in no mood for jokes. I glanced at a piece of paper he was holding. Something was afoot.

"Have a seat, Owen."

"I'll stand."

Something was definitely not right.

"Okay then, let's have it. What brings you up here? If it is about ruining your party, well…"

"It's about this." He handed me the paper which seemed to be the eye of his storm.

It took me a second to scan the photo. I recognized myself and an old friend and I also recognized The Ulysses Pub in Dublin. It was from my days at Trinity. I looked from the photo to Owen. He was glowering and my stomach was starting to squeeze.

"Okay, I see it. What is this all about, Owen?"

Two minutes later I had the story; at least his side of it. I was astounded at first, but then me wee mind began to grasp a few things. In fact, I was so relieved that I needed a drink to celebrate. I told Owen he could relax and I went into the kitchen to pour us each a dram of Jameson. In jelly glasses, of course. He was finally sitting on the couch when I returned.

"So you do know this guy, huh Des?"

I handed Owen his drink and parked my ass in the easy chair and crossed my legs.

"I knew him. Knew him quite well actually, but I have not seen Ali Halloran in years."

"That's his real name?"

"Yes, Ali Halloran and I grew up in the same neighborhood in Dublin. His dad was Irish and his mom was Moroccan, I believe. We teased him about being an Arab; called him The Sheik. Kid's stuff, really. He was an okay guy. Not the sort I would picture leading a bunch of bandits in Darfur." I paused. "And Sony Is sure that this guy is the same one who kidnapped her?"

"She is sure he is the guy," said Owen. "He does have a distinctive face. The nose and eyes."

"Ali is also about six foot five inches tall. Can she verify that?"

"She has said he was very tall."

"Well, let me see. There actually could be a connection, I suppose. Ali was another aspiring poet at Trinity. He was into Beckett while I was enthralled with O'Searcaigh...and of course, Roland Heinz. We both discovered Heinz at the same time when we took a class in poetic novelists. This would have been back maybe fifteen years ago or more."

"So he would have known everything about Roland? His family, too?"

"Look, Owen, I know what you are getting at."

"Before I 'get at' anything else I want to ask you man to man. Did you have anything to do with Sonia's kidnapping? This guy's face was caught on a security camera in the crowd when Sonia was shot at in Nairobi"

I was stunned by this bit of information, but absorbed it none the less. This 'man to man' form of oath cuts to the heart of an Irishman. I answered him with a clear conscience, "No."

Did you have anything to do with her ransom being paid?"

I hoped he didn't see the little flicker in my eye as I answered that one. Besides, he did not pose it 'man to man.'

"No," I lied.

It was a complicated tale that I had been sworn to never tell. I saw no advantage to breaking that oath now. Yes, I had a connection to a ransom paid for a girl I had never met before, but there was no urgent need to tell Dr. Palmer this part of the story. The fact that this same girl meant so much to me now was something else. It would all come out later, but I swallowed it for now with a Jameson chaser.

"Will you talk to this FBI agent?"

"The FBI is still poking around?"

"Since the shooting in Nairobi, yes."

"I will be happy to talk to anyone about my information."

"Thank you."

"So you believe me then?"

Owen stood and set his glass down on the coffee table. He had not touched it.

"I'm a pretty good judge of character, Des." He shook his head with his eyes closed. "I don't think you did or would do anything to hurt Sonia."

"That means a lot to me."

"Yes, but it only applies to the kidnapping."

I should have known this was coming.

"You're a married man with way more experience than she has. You've got her going in circles emotionally. Her mom and I don't see any future for you two unless you are free. Even then…"

The dangling 'then' spoke volumes.

"Tell Sony what I said, okay? Then you can tell her and her mother that I am leaving here as soon as my book events are finished. That should be in two weeks or so."

"That's probably for the best, Des."

I hated that condescending line. "Oh, fuck the best, man."

Owen started to walk out, but stopped. He didn't have to and probably shouldn't have, but like I said, he is a good man.

"I know a way out of hell," he said.

"Ben Kingley as Ghandi in the film?"

"Help the FBI, Des, and then figure out a way to get a divorce."

"That last part is not going to happen."

"Then just do the first part."

He left quietly. When I heard his truck start up and drive off I picked up his untouched Jelly glass and downed it in a gulp. I pulled an old musty afghan over my legs as the house had suddenly become very chilly. I wished I could be a fly on the wall down there at Ghost Farm when Owen reported in to the Costello women.

Despite of or because of the turns of the day I took up my notebook and wrote:

The morning sky is mottled
Fish scales in the ether
Like an icy pond that will not hold a skate
My eye is caught in the spaces
My mind rests on the islands
Got the feeling it's going to be a long wait
Because there is nothing behind the broken clouds
Nothing 'til forever

I let the notebook slide onto the floor and fell asleep.

CHAPTER TWENTY-THREE

BIM

"What's under that tarp anyway?" Mike asked as he nodded to the covered car which occupied half of my garage. I couldn't tell if he was really that curious about cars or if he was just trying to make conversation.

"You know anything about cars, Mike?"

"I know I like them. Especially old vintage muscle cars...like the one you've got here."

"How do you know what I got here? You peek under there already?"

"Naw, but the shape kind of gives it away. Low, wide, solid."

"That's pretty good."

"I should tell you that once upon a time I took a lot of those calendar shots of hot girls draped over the hoods of hot cars. Probably not the same vintage of yours, Bim, but it gave me an eye for cars."

"Go ahead and pull the tarp off," I said. I hadn't taken an interest in my old Chevy since the stroke. Seeing it always made me smile. Mike smiled too when the tarp came away.

"Wow! '68 or '69?"

"That my boy, is a '68 Chevelle Super Sport 396. Original blue paint and stripes. Go ahead and pop the hood."

Mike levered up the hood and did a low whistle. I had the original engine and I kept it clean, but with none of that showy chrome crap that others favor. I came from the original factory school. This Chevy was kept just the way I drove her off the lot all those years ago.

"I bought that car after saving my first year's paychecks at the quarry. I was just a kid back then and what you drove meant a lot around here. None of those sissy hybrids back in those days. You drove your mom's Ford until you could buy your own set of wheels."

"And then you went up and down Main on summer nights, right?"

"They did that in Boston, too, huh?"

"Pretty much. This sure is a beauty."

I had levered myself up into my walker and joined Mike at admiring the goods under the hood. "Hey, do me a favor and crank her up will you, Mike?"

"Where's the key?"

"Under the driver's side floor mat. I ain't started it since the stroke so it may take a few tries."

Mike got in and found the key. The 396 roared to life on the first try leaving some gray exhaust polluting the garage.

"Pull 'er out of there a bit."

Mike slipped the Hurst four-speed into first and eased the beast into the driveway. I signaled him to shut her down. He rolled down the window.

"What do you want to do?"

I was going to just sit in my chair and admire her for a while, but then a bright idea flashed in my head. "You wanna take 'er for a spin?"

Mike's smile answered the question. He started to get out to help me, but I waved him off and went around to the passenger side. The thought struck me that I had never sat in that seat before. Times change.

"We'd better blow out some of that stale gas, Mike," I said as he started her back up. I saw Pat standing in the back door and she was smiling, too. I waved at her and she waved back.

"Take a left and let's find a quiet country road." I glanced in the rearview mirror on my side and saw my wheelchair and walker in the garage. I was free again for a while.

Mike was a pretty good driver and we found a road where we could open her up a little bit. The old gas was making her knock so I told him we'd better find a gas station and get some high test in her veins. At the gas station, Mike was pumping while I fumbled through the glove box. I found the classic car registration that needed to be renewed, some vintage Wisconsin road maps, and a photo of myself taken with my car. When Mike got back in I handed it to him.

"Holy moley, Bim, when was that taken? That's you right?"

"I'm guessing not long after I got her. Maybe 1969."

"Nice ducktail."

I took the picture back to study it. "Yeah, I guess I was what you might call a greaser back in the day. Most of the car guys were. Every once in a while I still see hair like that in Fondy on some old fart who still has hair. It makes me nostalgic. Those were pretty good days back then."

"I suppose."

"Christ, Mike, you're here a couple weeks and you're 'supposing' already?"

"It's infectious."

"I suppose."

We shared a giggle as I let my mind wander back into that photograph.

"In 1969 I had already been working at the quarry for a couple a' two three years. Lot of guys around here were in Viet Nam. Some never came home. One guy who did was Roland Heinz. That's when I met him. His first day on the job at Schneider Stone they give him to me to train. The boss liked to turn the army vets into blasters cuz he figured they had been around explosives in the war. Well, Rollie didn't know shit, but he picked it up fast. Right off I knew he had something bugging him, though. He had seen some shit over there that he was keeping inside. I knew a few guys that came back bragging about the whole thing, but he wasn't talking."

"I knew you two were old friends," said Mike.

"Well, we became friends by hanging out after work. Drinking loosened him up. I got bits and pieces out of him in the bars. Then he got married to Karin Bollander and he got quiet again. Went straight home for a while."

I looked at Mike and smiled. "Id'a gone straight home to her, too. She was by far the prettiest girl around here. Her sister, Meg wasn't bad either."

"I know that part of the story."

"Yeah, that part and the end is pretty well known now, eh?"

"Lots has been written."

"Yep, after he got famous and dead."

I winced when I said those words. Roland was one of my few friends. Reading his books now was sometimes like spending time with him, but I missed the old days. I guess everybody misses their old days. Riding in my Chevy with Mike was bringing it all back and, as long as we were out…

"Hey Mike. Let's go get a beer."

I knew he knew what I was doing and, God bless him, he went along with it.

"Where to, Birn?"

"Back to town. Main Street. If I'm going to take a stroll through my past today, I might as well go all the way. Tipper's Tap. Near 4th Street. I got a taste for a pickled egg."

Mike had to help me navigate into Tipper's since I had left the walker at home. I felt kinda stupid being led in like I was smashed already, but I knew no one inside really cared. It was still early and the drinkers were there because they always were there at that time of day. I noticed the place had not changed much in years. Probably hadn't been cleaned much either. Nice atmosphere if you just wanted to get drunk and forget. Fortunately, I was there to remember. One or two beers would do.

"So you and Roland came in here?" Mike asked as two tap beers were set on cardboard coasters in front of us at the bar.

"We hit a lot of spots back then, but this one was closest to where we both lived."

"Ah, the neighborhood bar."

"Yeah, the place where the same six guys were always sitting here no matter what time you came in. The TV was black and white back then and guys mostly just watched game shows and yelled at the screen."

My pickled egg arrived on a napkin.

"There was some sort of comfort in walking into a place like this after work and feeling the camaraderie of fellow drinkers winding down their day. Besides the retired guys who sat here all day, we were mostly blue collar guys on the way home. It was nice back then."

Mike was listening closely like a houseguest is supposed to.

"At some point Roland started staying a little too long in these joints. He didn't go home until later. I figured him and Karin were having problems, but you didn't ask about stuff like that. I was still single so I had no one to go home to. I didn't mind that he stayed out."

I ate the egg and downed the beer. Mike gestured to the bartender to refill us both.

"Then one day, I think it might have been in this very bar, he started to tell me stuff. He told me about Nam and some of the killing he had seen. Said it changed him and he didn't know how to deal with it. Said it was fucking up his marriage and he didn't know how to deal with that either. I remember he started crying. Not loud or anything like that, but a sort of tearless sobbing that shook his big body up and down."

"That's sad."

"Yeah, and then I wouldn't see him after work for a while. I figured him and his wife were patching it up. He never said anything at the quarry, just did his work. Then he quit and he was gone. Heard she moved out on him and he moved to the Holyland."

"And we know the rest of the story, huh Bim?"

I liked Mike. I could see why Carrie took off and married him. He was smart and a good companion. He seemed truly compassionate listening to me ramble on about my past and Roland's. I didn't have the heart to tell him he didn't know shit about Roland Heinz. You could read the books, even shake his big hand, but until you put all the pieces together you didn't know the man.

I was pretty much talked and pooped out by the time we got home. Mike returned to his endless phone calls in the house and I got comfortable in the garage. I wanted to nap, but something about the day kept me thinking. All the talk about Roland had me focused on not only the past, but some stuff that I knew was about to happen.

CHAPTER TWENTY-FOUR

SONIA

I was in the second week of my self-imposed exile to the writing studio. Mom and Owen knew I was escaping to think things over and left me pretty much alone. I guess I had accepted Owen's assessment that Des was telling the truth about his involvement with this Ali Assan character, but the fact that they knew each other still creeped me out to the point I could not see or talk to him. He had stopped trying to phone me a week ago so now we were locked into some sort of a silent game of chicken.

I was finished with the FBI for now. Delforte said he would keep the file open, which even I knew meant they had nothing going. I knew trying to find that shooter would be like looking for a needle in a haystack in Kenya. Ali had disappeared, too, back down the rabbit hole he had emerged from. Delforte said he was most likely an Irish troublemaker who used his education and Arab blood to make money selling weapons and bullshit to the Darfur bandits. It seems Ali went by many names and turned up in many places. I only hoped one of those places was not Pipe, Wisconsin. Delforte thought that seemed unlikely. He was on a watch list and his physical characteristics would make him easy to filter out.

For some reason I was not worried about the shooter. Those guys never traveled. The problem was that I could not return to Nairobi and my school. I had good people running the place and my support would continue, but if I could not go back there without fearing for my life, then why go back? Maybe that was the motive for the whole thing. Keep the little American do-gooder out of a place she did not belong. Anyway, that's how warped my thinking had gotten since I learned Des was involved. I really wanted to talk to him and that desire grew daily, but it was an itch without a scratch. I was afraid he was going to lie to me and I could not have taken that kind of betrayal from him.

At first I decided to escape into my writing, but not much was coming out. In fact I found myself sort of re-writing some poems I had already written just after my kidnapping. When I wrote now I substituted Des' face for Ali's. There were a lot of wads of yellow legal pad paper in the trash. There were a lot of deleted word documents on my computer. I turned to Roland for guidance.

In The Needle's Eye, he wrote mostly about the third incarnation of Garnet Granger: the third dream of death and confrontation with The Swift Sure Hand. Of course, Roland's dreamscapes were many-layered, but if you hunted around and turned over the words you could find the insight you wanted to find. I found what I needed in Chapter 17:

She felt fear. Fear like midnight. Fear like electron death. She was alone inside her skin, which meant that not even the cosmic void was present; no stars, no moon, no light to walk toward. And yet she willed herself to move. She wished she could sit down and cry, but there was no place to sit and no tears to wash her face. The only thing alive was her fear and it was a strong presence: a sucking drain that drew her into a dark spiral away from the boney hand she sought.

She thought she was dead and yet, how could she think if she was gone. In the dark her skin hair bristled to a subtle movement. It was not a hand that passed across her skin, but rather the draft of the wing of an unseen bird. If fear was a bird she was not afraid because anything with wings meant love. Gravity was fear, flight was Him.

She felt the waft again. It was circling her. A feather touched her face. She turned her head upward and waited for the next pass. When it came she smiled in the darkness and suddenly a light came on. The hand on the switch by the door was her mother's. Though long dead, her mother was the hand, the wing, the light.

"Leave the light on, Momma," she said and then dropped her head backward into a pillow of stars and a dream within a dream.

Boy, that Garnet Granger sure liked to sleep. I checked my cell phone just in case Des had tried to call again. The ringer was off all the time now. Of course, he hadn't, but there was a message from Carrie. I listened to her voice mail. She was reaching out her hand in the dark to me. I decided to call her back and return the gesture. We made a date for lunch in the Holyland the next day. With the end of my exile in sight, I walked into the house and plunked down on the couch next to Mom and Owen who were watching the late news. They observed and honored my silence, but I got smiles and a thigh pat. I had walked back into their light.

Carrie picked me up the next day and we headed out into the land up and east of The Ledge. I was now late September and the trees were starting to turn color in the clumps of forest that survived amidst the farms. The day was perfect: just enough clouds to make the sky seem even bluer than it was. When I was little I thought God sat on clouds like these and looked down on us and protected us. Today it felt like He was still there. After all we were in The Holylands.

Carrie knew a little bar and grill near St. Cloud that was a converted mill next to a stream. We arrived just before noon and were the only customers until a few construction guys and farmers' wives arrived a little while later. We sat by the window. Carrie looked out at the day. I looked at Carrie. She was still a fairy princess to me. The most beautiful face I had ever seen. Helen of Troy was a drab compared to Carrie Stirling Gabler.

"How are they doing?" I asked. We had not talked about Pat and Bim yet.

Carrie's eyes came back into the room and locked glacier blue on me. "You know, Sony, they are actually doing great. I mean, both of them have huge health issues, but there is a serenity in that house now that I never felt before. Go figure, huh?"

"Bad stuff can bring people together," I said. I didn't sigh when I said it, but I might have done it with my eyes.

"But, not for you and Des, right?"

"I am thinking about cutting it off forever. We should just move on."

"Is it because of this latest stuff or his wife?"

My eyebrows shot up. Carrie had a way of getting right down to it. Well, I figured that was why she called me. Bloody Marys for truth serum and those eyes to cut away the crap.

"I know you know all about the photo of him I got. Something still isn't right about that, but yeah, it is the wife that lies at the heart of the matter. She is never going away."

Carrie nodded. We both sipped our drink. The dill pickle spear instead of a stalk of celery and the little beer chaser were local trademarks. I ate my pickle and waited for her to say something.

"How long do you expect to live, Sony?"

That was not the question I had expected.

"Huh?"

"Well, you are what, twenty-three, twenty-four now?"

"Twenty-three."

"And Des is how old?"

"Forty-two."

"So he's already twenty-one years down the road ahead of you."

"That's the math."

"The way I see it those years are important, but not as important as minutes."

I could only listen and shake my head slightly meaning I didn't understand.

"Okay, listen. Everything to do with love is measured in minutes. The human heart is a clock without a face, but it does keep time."

"In minutes?"

"Yep, forget the freaking years. I am only going to keep talking if you tell me you love Des. Otherwise this is useless. We should just order lunch."

Love or lunch? "You tell me, Carrie. I think about him when I wake up and always just before I fall asleep. All the time in between I see his face. But, then when I am actually with him I tend to be pissed off at him. I want him to do something besides court me. Like move heaven and earth and get free from his wife."

"Okay, you're in love. Good. Lunch can wait." This statement was served with a smile that was as warm as the sun coming through the glass. When Carrie's penetrating eyes were accompanied by her smiling mouth you just had to respond. Indeed, she was a fairy princess.

"Say for now," she continued, "that nothing ever changes. He stays married in name only and he is linked to your other incident. Does any of that really change how you feel this minute? Or a minute from now? Or a thousand minutes from now?"

I drank my chaser.

"One minute of real love is worth more than anything else. If you guys have found that real love...well then..." She picked up her drink and hoisted it in a toast. "God bless you."

"But it's all so complicated..."

Her eyes changed color as she shook her head. "No, Sonia, it's all so simple. When you figure that out you will be much happier. I asked you how long you expect to live. The correct answer is unknowable, but you can manage the next minute, right?. And maybe the next?"

It might have been the Bloody Mary, but I felt some sort of immediate release of my tension. I knew Carrie had nailed me. I projected my life too far into the future all the time. Most people do. It would be a hard switch to flip, but not impossible. We both ordered Reuben sandwiches and never talked about Des again that day. After lunch we moved to the bar and had the best session of pure girl talk that I had enjoyed in ages. Mom and Melanie were good talkers, but we knew each other too well to really dish the dirt. Carrie was the perfect companion and I enjoyed our day one minute at a time.

CHAPTER TWENTY-FIVE

DESMOND

Well, I had told everyone I was going to leave town, but I was not moving too far or too fast. I did a lovely book signing event in Madison at a quaint college bookstore that reminded me of some funky places in the UK or Ireland. It seems Madison still had some poetry-loving hippies hanging about. And they actually knew who I was and knew my poems. They shouted my lines back at me when I read and almost carried me out to their pubs when I had finished. Almost. Interest in my book events was usually an hour of triumph followed by a long night of defeat. This store sold four or five books. I dutifully signed them and went to the motel room. I began to think about actually returning to Limerick and what that would mean. I called Cedric out of boredom.

"Ced, hello. What's going on back there?"

"Where are you, Desmond?"

"Still in Wisconsin. You know where I am."

"Let me see, today you are in Madison signing books at Plowshare Books."

"I was there. I did sign books."

Something was going on. I heard Cedric shuffling papers. He asked me to hang on a second. I lay back on the bed and waited. I felt some slight tension beginning to tighten my stomach.

"You still there, Des?"

"Talk to me."

"Okay, a couple things. I have some correspondence here for you. Some mail actually"

"And you opened it actually?"

"Of course."

"Go on."

"Three items. One. A letter from the FBI in America. Their investigation of the Costello shooting in Nairobi, blah blah blah…no longer has any interest in you."

"That's nice. What did you substitute with your 'blahs?'"

"Just some legalese blather."

I thought to myself that practically no one on earth had any interest in me these days. Motel rooms cultivate those thoughts. "Well, I suppose that is good news, but I already had that information from the agent. That photo with me in it was mere coincidence. Old news."

"Yes, well perhaps, but that brings me to item number two."

I raised my head off the pillow and sat up. I didn't think I was going to like item number two. "What?"

"You received a letter that had been forwarded from your old address in Dublin. I noticed the postmark was Cairo. It had been mailed three weeks ago so I figured I had better open it since you were…"

"You opened it because you are a snoop," I interrupted. "Go on."

"It's a single type-written page with a phone number and the initials 'A.H.'"

So up pops the devil. I knew who it was and I had rather half-expected the contact. The question now was should I even respond to this obvious request to speak to him? "Give me the number, Ced." I wrote it down. "Where is that prefix code from?"

"Actually, it's a prepaid mobile number in right here in the UK."

"Did you do a reverse look up?"

"Yes, that's how I knew it was mobile and unlisted."

"Okay, I got that. What else?"

"You're not going to tell me who it is?"

"Fuck it, man, you already know. What else is on your docket?"

I could hear Cedric chuckling, which annoyed the hell out of me. I was now up and pacing the room.

"Ah, well, perhaps I saved the best for last."

The FBI and Ali Halloran. Who could top them on a list of people I didn't want to hear from? "Get to it, asshole."

"Number three is a letter with the letterhead of a law firm in Dublin."

I switched the phone to my other ear as if enough bad news had entered the other. I knew Ced would save the biggest bombshell for his finale.

"The law offices of Stein, Shay, and O'Shay wish to inform you that our client....who remains nameless..., but you know who...is petitioning you for a dissolution of marriage. Blah, blah, blah. Paperwork to follow, etc, etc."

I listened to those words and didn't know whether I was going to drop onto the floor or fly through the ceiling. It had to be a trick. A sick joke. Isn't that how unexpected great news is always received? With suspicion and doubt. Whatever it was my heart rate was speeding up and I was instantly light-headed. I had to sit back down.

"You still there, Des?"

"This is not a joke, right Ced? You know I would fly home and kill you instantly."

"Turn on your computer. A photo copy is already in your email. Save it. Print it and go out and have a pint or two."

"She is actually doing this? What have you heard? You know every other bloody thing."

"Well, I did hear a little something about a wealthy Fianna Fail representative to the Irish House sweeping the wife of a wayward poet off her feet. It seems your biggest enemy has become your best friend."

"Huh?"

"Cupid! The little bastard doesn't give a rat where he aims his arrows. He probably got tired of riddling your sorry ass and turned on her."

I was already up at the desk and into my email, reading the letter.

"Jaysus, Mary, and Saint Joseph! There it is!"

"Listen, old man, I have some other business to take care of. Enjoy the moment, okay? Ciao."

Ced was off and I was left sitting there re-reading the letter over and over. What to do? How to celebrate? The possibilities were endless. But, then reality eventually delivers a sobering slap in the face. I wanted to call Sony, but it struck me that this sort of news should be given in person and I was not sure she would even see me. I would need to work on that. And then there was the specter of my old mate, Ali Halloran standing in the corner. He wanted a call from me. I didn't like the idea of phoning him even if the FBI was no longer interested in me, but I knew whatever he wanted to tell me had something to do with Sony. I suddenly felt the ropes of entanglement tightening around my new happy heart. There was business to take care of and I didn't know where to begin besides making that call.

I poured myself a half a glass of Jameson and drank half of that. I stared at the number I had copied from Ced and tried to divine something from the numbers. They were only numbers arranged by chaos and I stepped into that void with my fingertips.

The phone I was calling sounded distant and tinny when it rang up. I let it ring perhaps six times and was ready to push the red button when it was answered. Well, I thought, this is going to be interesting.

"Yes?" said the voice.

"Ali?"

"Desmond?"

"Yes, what do you want?"

"Des, I had given up on you."

"What do you want?"

"I don't see you much in the news anymore. No photos in magazines"

"Yeah, well, I've been seeing pictures of you."

"You are referring to that incident in Nairobi."

"Yeah."

"Of course, security cameras are everywhere these days. You know why I was there, right?"

"I know, but you didn't do a very good job."

"Maybe I did more than you know."

"Meaning what?"

"Meaning she is now safe."

"Assurances?"

"Only my word."

"Jaysus, there's a thin broth served."

"Well, sorry, but that is the only reason I wanted to speak to you. I thought it was important that you know our business is over."

"And you're absolutely sure about that?"

"Okay, Des, listen to me. Use the internet. Find a copy of the Nairobi News for August 24, this year. Go to page four about halfway down the page. If you make the logical assumptions then you should have your answer."

I was taking notes.

"I'll do that."

"Good."

"Anything else?"

"I miss our old days of poetry and Guinness. I wish we could talk like that again."

"Time passes."

"Yes it does."

"Goodbye, Ali."

"Farewell…"

There was hint of sadness in his voice. I thought he had more to say, but he was gone. I immediately went in search of that newspaper article. I found it where he said it would be. I saved the information and closed the notebook just as the phone buzzed. Caller ID said it was Sony.

"Hello, girl."

"Hi, Des, do you have a minute?"

CHAPTER TWENTY-SIX

MOLLY

Melanie and Ray arrived at Ghost Farm about the time as the first snow, which came early this year. Early autumn had been mild and pleasant, but November had flipped a switch sending us into a period of clear, cold days and nights of light snow. Owen paid quite a bit of attention to the weather and he said it was because the jet stream had dipped down and was flowing almost right above us, sucking cold air out of Canada and drawing moisture out of the southwest. As anyone knows, weather is the number one conversation starter in Wisconsin. Everything else follows its lead, but in my house, the weather was a distant second to the baby, whose presence was now more than a bump in my daughter's tummy.

Melanie's husband Ray had taken a three month leave of absence from his law firm to come back to Fond du Lac. The combination of his wife's pregnancy and his grandmother's illness brought him home. As you know, he is a successful entertainment lawyer in Los Angeles and I figured he would be antsy and bored around our farm, but I was pleasantly surprised to find him relaxed and interested in the quiet life.

Yes, life was again quiet at Ghost Farm. The film crew of summer was gone and Sonia and Des had settled into something of a détente regarding their relationship. Des continued to live in Meg's old house on The Ledge and Sony was still spending her nights with us, but there was definitely a change. When Des flew back to Ireland last weekend I knew that it was to be present for his final divorce hearing. I don't think his presence was required, but Sonia told me that he needed to be a witness to his freedom. She was excited, but trying to hide it. I was on the periphery of their affairs and Owen often reminded me to stay there. Anyway, he and I had our own plans.

Mel and Ray spent quite a bit of time in town with the Stouffers. After all they were family, too. Pat was doing well and was finished with the chemotherapy. She had had at least two radiation treatments, I think, and everyone's expectations were high for her all clear. Bim was Bim, of course, but he did seem to enjoy the company of Ray in the garage and Mike, too, when he was in town. Carrie and Mel had become great friends.

I tend to hold my breath as I write this. Everything is going well right now, but I am a natural worrier. Right now I am watching Owen read the paper and drink coffee in the kitchen. I had my computer between us, but we keep stealing glances at each other. Now he is chuckling to himself.

"What is it, honey?" I asked. I didn't think it was about me.

"Just reading Bim's latest column. What a hoot."

"What's he up to this week?"

"He is attacking what he refers to as the 'idlers' who hang out at the Main St Quick Market. He says the same six coots occupy the only table in the store and nurse the free cup of coffee all morning while scratching lotto tickets."

"I've seen those guys. They are there every day."

"Yeah, but take away the store and substitute the garage. Take away the coffee and make it beer and you have Bim making fun of himself."

"Maybe that is his intention."

"I doubt it."

"Doubt what?" asked Melanie as she came into the kitchen in her robe and wool socks. She reminded me so much of days gone by when she and her sister would come downstairs full of curiosity and sleepy sand in their eyes.

"We were discussing Bim's column in the paper, honey," I said as I got up to get her some coffee.

"Oh yeah, Pat sends us the clippings every week even though we can read them online."

"You slept in today, Hon."

"Sony and I were up late last night yacking."

Right on cue the backdoor opened and Sony sleep-walked in.

"Coffee, must have," Sonia muttered robotically.

I poured everyone a cup and started a fresh pot.

"I'm glad you both are here," I said and caught Owen's eye. He knew the segue line and so did the girls.

Melanie yelled to Ray who was in the living room watching Sportcenter. "Honey, get in here."

Was I so predictable? When everyone was seated with a cup in front of them I went around to Owen and placed my hands on his shoulders.

"We set a date," I said and watched the smiles come out of the kids.

"Woo hoo!" exclaimed Sony.

"'Bout time," said Mel.

"When?" asked Ray.

"Well, we are getting married here, actually in the barn, on Black Friday, the day after Thanksgiving."

Sony: "Black Friday? Why not Thanksgiving? Mel and I will be shopping that day."

"Very funny," I said. "We could not get a preacher to come out here on the holiday so we are going for the next day. I hope you can squeeze a short ceremony into your shopping plans."

"Congratulations," said Ray.

"Will you be best man?" asked Owen. Ray nodded his approval.

"What are we, flower girls?" Sonia quipped.

"Actually you guys are maid and matron of honor."

"For a quickie wedding?" said Mel with a grin. "When do we get fitted for the pink Little Bo Peep dresses?'

"Yeah," said Sony, "we need to make hair appointments to get bee-hived."

I loved the scene. No one was sleepy anymore. The coffee kicked in and it felt more like a celebration than any formal banquet at a supper club. Amidst all the happy talk and joshing of me and Owen, I sat at the table and had a very strong sense of Roland's presence. Of course, I did; it was his house, his table, his cornflower coffee cups and plates. It was also his master plan that allowed this day to happen. I had a good feeling that he had written this chapter long ago and we were all in place between his pages. His words come to life.

Our wedding preparations were pretty simple. Get everyone together, get a preacher to make it legal, and say the words that need to be said. We decided on the barn for the ceremony because that was where Owen's and my story began. I found him when our family owl got sick. More than that, there could be no other place that was holier for us in the entire Holyland.

The part of the barn that had been kept as a museum for Roland's life and work was very much a cathedral. I have described how the light is allowed in through natural openings in the roof to create a sublime mood for the space below. The room is not particularly clean: old hay is still in the mow and there are always going to be critters making a home there. But, there is a smell of rural sanctity that reminds me so much of my father. It was here he was tuned into the cosmos, as he used to say. I wanted him tuned into my wedding, too. I was never too spiritual before I came to live here. Now I spend half my time in the two worlds of the Here and the There. Once I accepted that, my writing flourished. I became Roland's daughter in every way.

Besides the simple wedding, we had booked a big table at Yelanek's Supper Club in Jericho for after the ceremony. Since Thanksgiving dinner was going to be at Pat and Bim's I had gotten out of cooking for the holiday weekend. Yippee! I was going to be a bride! The fact that I was now fifty-five was only a footnote. I felt like I was twenty-five again. Woot!

CHAPTER TWENTY-SEVEN

DESMOND

I have been playing around with the idea of finally writing the name of my now ex-wife. It is still not coming easily to my fingertips or lips despite the fact that she was cordial during our brief meeting at the courthouse in Dublin. I even shook hands with her very proper politician beau. Nice man and good luck to him. I was more than happy to hand _____ off to him so we could all go our merry ways. Hah, I am an ass!

Cedric had driven up with me from Shannon and I enjoyed even his sardonic company in the car to freedom. I think having a tall, gay black man with me left the new guy with the wrong impression, but I certainly didn't care. My mind was halfway around the world as we stepped out into the rainy streets.

"I suppose now we are going to have another wedding," drolled Cedric.

"Who said anything about that?" I replied as I popped open an umbrella.

"Wasn't that the primary goal of your desire to be free of....the other?"

"Freedom indeed presents all sorts of possibilities, Ced. The truth is Sonia and I have never discussed marriage."

"Never?"

"Never as it related to us."

"Well, I…"

"Besides, you are prying, man. No more for now. Let's find a pint."

I knew where I wanted to have that pint and it was only a short ride to The Ulysses. It being early in the day, we had no problem occupying the exact same places at the rail where Ali and I had been photographed years ago. You see, I have this one little quirk in my personality. I always need to close loops when I can. That photograph had started a loop that I now was closing off with Ced and Guinness. I drank to it silently.

"So what *is* your next move, if I may ask?" inquired Cedric with his new foam mustache.

"The question of the day," I replied.

"I would say."

I took another swallow of sweet, dark Ireland. The stuff that came in a can in the States was nowhere close to this ambrosia. It was like the kiss of an old lover. Something to be savored and then maybe forgotten.

"Did you know that I am living in the house where Roland Heinz's old lover lived?"

Ced shook his head.

"She hated his innards, too, I should add. But, it is odd how those two emotions seem to hang in the air in that old farm house. Meg Bollander was her name. The sister of Roland's wife, Karin who left him for another man. The very dust in that place crackles with pain. Heartache. I find it hard to explain. You would have to sit in her chair at night and see the moon set into Lake Winnebago like a lost gold coin. I can actually feel her utter anguish."

"It sounds ghastly."

"Hah, you would say that. What I feel is a creative nudge that I have never felt before in those rooms. I not only feel her urge to create art from pain, but I also feel the presence of Roland Heinz. She sucked his spirit into the house with her vacuum of loathing."

"I won't pretend to understand you, but I surmise you are getting some writing done."

"Yes. Lots and lots of it."

"Another book of poetry for Stompe Publishing? Have they seen it? I haven't heard a thing,"

"No, they haven't read a word, Ced. But, they will."

"When?"

I chuckled. "In due time. But, they won't just be getting a book of poetry."

I saw Cedric's head come up in the mirror across from us. I saw him turn to me. Unflappable Ced was flapping.

"What did you say? I'm confused."

"Not just a poetry book, my friend."

I let that statement hang in the pub like an ale advert on the wall. Ced was trying to figure out what new trick this old dog had learned in America.

"It's titled *Above Galilee* and it is my first novel."

'But, but…are you a novelist now?"

"It seems I am. Or will be when Stompe publishes it."

Cedric's eyebrows were again knitted in consternation. Perhaps he was considering becoming the agent of a new novelist rather than an over-the-hill poet. Either way, it was testing his faith in me.

"Can I see chapters?" he asked, which didn't surprise me.

I reached into my pocket and produced a flash drive. I handed it to him. "Here, do your job as my agent and get some interest stirred up. I have a feeling Stompe will be interested in this. Now be sure to get a nice advance. I'll sign nothing without one and a new contract will have nothing to do with me as a poet. Got that?"

"You just got an advance on a poetry book. I got you that ten thousand only three months ago."

"The poetry book for which I was advanced is on that drive also. There are also pictures on that drive of myself and Sonia. Me and Molly Costello. Me and Sarah Dylan. All taken by Mike Gabler. Cedric, I have just handed you a gold mine. Go to Stompe and start working it."

I saw him look at the flash key and close his hand over it. Ced was nothing if not a quick one on the uptake.

"How soon do you want me to move on this, Des?"

"Yesterday."

He nodded, put the flash in his pocket, and finished his beer. "Let's go," he said.

Ced and I decided to fly back to the US together. From JFK we would split up; he to Boston and Stompe Publishing and me to Pipe, Wisconsin and Sony. On the plane we sat side by side as he read my novel on his laptop. I tried not to look at him or read his expressions. That was making me crazy. He was, in fact, my first reader. Not even Sony knew that I had been up to this. No one knew. Well, perhaps the spirit of Meg Bollander knew and most certainly the ghost of Roland Heinz.

Somewhere over the Atlantic, Ced closed the lid of his notebook. I had mercifully fallen asleep as he read on. He gave me a soft nudge with his elbow. When my eyes opened he leaned into me and whispered my first review into my ear.

"Bloody fucking good shit, Des. Amazing."

"You think so?"

"Leave it to you to screw your life around. You are a way better novelist that you ever were a poet. I won't have any trouble selling this."

"Really?" I sounded like a praised child.

"Yes, really. I would like to see these Wisconsin Holy-lands some day. The way you describe it is ethereal. Reluctant modernism and rustic ritual all hidden away in a landscape populated by amazingly unique characters. It takes me back to Thackeray with a touch of Dickens. I loved every word of it. But, I am still stumped as to how this all came pouring out of you. You must have written this in what, three months?"

"Less actually, once I got going."

"Okay, I see you in this haunted house. You begin a poem, but then something happens. What for God's sake?"

Ced had set up the moment perfectly. I had no problem remembering the night I began to write in prose. I had gone to sleep in the old chair facing the picture window with a bit of a hangover that needed service. I had run out of Jameson and it was too late to go out. I rummaged around the Bollander cupboard looking for something to drink. I was angry at myself that night and wanted punishment. I found it in a bottle labeled Vermox. I sniffed it. Phew. Rot gut whiskey with maybe vermouth to make it even more bitter. Some sort of weed rested in the poison for what, flavor? Jaysus!

I drank a glass of the shit and almost vomited. Almost. Having been inoculated I downed another shot. And another. My blood turned to lava, but I was awake and full of energy. I took the bottle to the chair and opened my computer. I started a fresh word document and had intended to write a ditty about this new libation of the devil. As I flexed my fingers I looked out the window. I could see my face vaguely lit by the laptop screen. Beyond that reflection I saw lights along the far shore of the lake. I began to ponder the lake. The lake and The Ledge dominated this place. Above the lake and behind The Ledge lay The Holylands.

I saw the dog-earred copy of The Tap Root sitting on the coffee table that Ms. Bollander had left behind. Before I typed one line of verse I heard a voice in my head. It was a strong male voice and I knew whose it was. It could only be him.

"You can write your poems in prose."

And then that voice seemed to hand my mind over to another. It was not a ghost, but a feminine voice I knew very well. I wouldn't share that with Cedric.

I turned back to Cedric just as our descent into New York was being announced.

"Yes, the house was haunted, Ced. One of the spirits gave me a nudge."

"Naturally. Which one?"

"There were two, actually. A married couple. Meg and Roland Vermox. Lovely pair."

CHAPTER TWENTY-EIGHT

BIM

Somehow I always preferred Thanksgiving to Christmas. I think it may have something to do with less hype and more food. I had the second football game on out in the garage, and because of the temperature folks were pretty much leaving me alone. Of course, I have a dandy space heater going full blast and the little TV is a nice touch. Who cares if it's that damned Dallas playing? Gives me someone to root against. Besides, the house is full today. We have all the Costello girls over with their mates as well as our own houseguests, Carrie and Mike. Now, I have a little bet with myself on who's going to be the first one to come out here to escape. Hah, the back door is opening and here comes the Irishman in his jacket and gloves. I win.

"Mind if I join you, Bim?" Des O'Conner asked very politely.

"Grab a seat, Des, I've been expecting you."

"Ah then," he said as he took a seat, "This is quite cozy, isn't it?"

My opening. "Just like you and Sonia."

"And what exactly does that mean?"

"You tell me, boyo." I think I had him going.

"I pray you are not going to start that cradle robbing crap."

I slapped my knee and laughed. "No, no, you get a young'n then good for you. There's a pint of brandy in that paint can over there if you want a nip."

Des got up and found the bottle and took a bite out of it.

"American football, eh?"

"We're in America."

"Yeah, so it seems."

"Hey, listen, we should can the small talk, okay? We may not have much time to chat out here."

"Right."

The conversation I am about to chronicle was top secret when we had it, but things have changed since so I am going to share it.

"I think you have some news for me."

Des nodded and unfolded a piece of paper. It was a copy of a page from a newspaper. I studied it with great interest.

"Okay, Des, fill me in. What exactly does this mean?"

"Well, as you can see it is article is from the Nairobi News dated last summer. The picture shows a burned out VW bus, but you can still read the plates."

"I see that."

"A man's body was found in the van. We know who he was, too. He was the guy who took a shot at our girl."

"And you're sure?"

"Well, I am no detective, but this was sent to me for one reason only. And we both know by whom and why."

I folded up the paper and handed it back to Des.

"Gimme a hit of that brandy," I said. He did and I did. "So, our mutual friend is offering this up as proof that this problem is solved?"

"Yes."

"And we're buying that?"

"Yes."

"Why?"

"Okay, this dead man was the Darfur bandit who got burned by our...friend. It was he who swore to avenge his betrayal. Ali tracked him down and almost found him too late, but he found him. How that discovery led to this burned out van with a corpse is something I don't want to know."

"Me either. I just want to know all of this bullshit is over."

"I believe it is."

I looked that Irishman straight in the eye. We had a little history from a few years ago as you can tell and I have grown to trust him.

"Des, I can't do much from this garage. And after the stroke I can do even less. What goes on in this wide world beyond my driveway might as well be happening on the moon. I was given a trust a long time ago and I tried to do my part. If that part is over with then I am satisfied and maybe even a little happy."

"You were our only hope, Bim."

"Looks like it. Not that I ever wanted to be. Can we close this book?"

"It's closed," Des said in that Irish way that makes me believe it is truly closed.

"Then we won't talk about this anymore."

"I will probably have to tell Sony one of these days."

"Why?"

"There should be no secrets between us."

I could only shake my head. "You poets live on secrets and you always will. Got your own little code, too. Spies of the heart."

"Roland said that."

Ah, yes...Roland!

So that business was done. Good. The next thing was Molly's wedding. She had asked me to give her away, which was a task I really enjoyed. Handing her over in that barn to Owen was the nicest thing I had done since I handed myself over to Pat in Las Vegas. Having a wedding in a barn appealed to me. It was simple and quick. Hell, in my mind they had been married for years, but folks love their cere- monies, which included dinner. Of course, I despise Yelanek's Supper Club, but the giver of hands must attend the post-marital feast. At least they make a good Old Fash- ioned in that dump.

I should probably tell you why I don't like Yelanek's. It has to do with an incident that occurred years ago with my first wife. Like everyone else we used to go out there on Friday nights for the fish fry. You wait at the bar for an hour and get oiled before stumbling to a table for food you don't even want by then. Well, on one Friday night my wife and I are finally served our food as the snow is piling up outside. I keep telling her to hurry up and eat or we won't make it home.

Anyway, to make a long story short, she chokes on a fish bone. I see her eyes get real big as she gasps for breath. Then they roll up into her head and she falls off her chair onto the floor. I was stunned. Couldn't move. People are screaming. Chaos erupts. As it was, there were a bunch of EMT's in the room and a couple of them come over and start working on the old lady. They prop her up and do a Heimlich on her and out pops the fish bone attached to a sliver of fish. She still needs some resuscitation and, though she was coming back fast, I thought the whole thing had lasted for hours. I talked them out of calling an ambulance. No need for that, right? I mean she was talking away about walking into the light and all that for cry-eye. Anyway, on the way home she starts into me about not saving her myself. She goes on and on about how the last thing she saw was me just sitting in my chair doing nothing. Fifteen crappy miles crawling along in a snow storm listening to her bitching. She was lucky to be alive and all she could do was blame me for the whole evening.

I had thought about suing Yelanek's for that fish bone. What I really wanted to do was sue the paramedics for bringing her back. I did neither, but I swore I would never return to the scene of the crime. Now I was back for Molly's wedding dinner. I took Pat's hand under the table and squeezed it. After I married her I had secretly learned CPR from a book at the library. They still had good Old Fashioneds at the place. I even thought I recognized a couple old waitresses from the old days. I hoped they didn't recognize me.

I stayed mostly out of the table talk. I like to listen to people and I can tell a lot about them from how they converse after a couple drinks. This was a good bunch of people; no one out of line or mouthing off. Owen and Molly were too special for anyone to try to upstage them. Each person at the table was balanced by their counterpart. Mel and Ray. Carrie and Mike. Sony and Des. Molly and Owen. The luckiest man on earth and Patsy Stouffer.

I did notice that Des would not make eye contact with me. That was okay, we had a secret, but for now I just wanted to enjoy the wedding cake and the old lady in the corner who was playing some nice crap on an old Hammond organ. She and I were dying breeds, I thought. Next thing I knew I was the one on the floor at Yelanek's. Stroke number two had arrived like a bright light. Somewhere my ex was enjoying herself.

In the hospital, I learned that I was lucky. Already knew that. This stroke was a small one and there appeared to be not much more damage to my abilities. Well, I sort of ruined the wedding, but Pat said I was forgiven by Molly and Owen. Once they knew I was okay they had headed off on their honeymoon to New Mexico.

When I came home three days later, I was supposed to stay in the house. Bullshit! I wanted the serenity of the garage. Pat understood. She knew very well how priorities are arranged by illness. It was getting colder and darker earlier in the garage, but I was back. I kind of knew the next stroke would probably take me down for the count. I watched Pat and Carrie doing the dishes in the kitchen window and really didn't care about what happened as long as they were there in the soft light.

And by the way, the writing part of my life is nearly done. I can barely keep this journal now. Neither hand is dexterous enough for that. But I am reading books like the pages are my lifelines. I have this feeling that I am missing something that I really need to know. Funny how a stroke that slows down your body makes your brain go into high gear.

CHAPTER TWENTY-NINE

SONIA

I am so glad Mom and Owen got off on their honeymoon. The scene at Yelanek's sure put a damper on all the happiness. Bim was awake when they rolled him out of the supper club on a gurney and I saw him say something to Mom. I asked her what he said before we all left and she told me that he said he always wanted to go to New Mexico and to have a good time. I cried all the way home as Des tried to console me.

"He'll be okay, Sony. It's a good sign that he was awake and talking."

"God, I hope so. But, Mom. Her wedding ending like that."

We pulled up to Ghost Farm in Des's car and stopped in the turn around by the studio. I wanted to invite him in, more to keep comforting me than anything else, but I just couldn't do it. Despite his divorce we still had issues. It was mostly me this time.

"Your mom and Owen have been happy together for a long time. Nothing that happened today is going to change that. It was just bad luck come to call is all."

Mel and Ray pulled in behind us and I watched them go into the house. My sister still couldn't stand Des and made no pretenses about it. Des shook his head as he watched her scowling.

"Jaysus, Sony, you keep me at arms length and your sister hates me guts. What am I to do to please you?"

"I don't know. Just give it some time. Both of us. All of us."

"Speaking of time, have you found enough to read my manuscript?"

Des had given me a hard copy of his novel and so far all I had done with it was stare at it. That pile of paper was like a brick wall set between us and I wasn't exactly sure why.

"I'm going to get to it tonight."

He nodded.

"I'll call you later," I said as I opened the car door to get out.

He just nodded again. I was going to say something else, but I thought because of his silence he was pouting. I shut the door that I wanted to slam very slowly and headed into the studio. Des turned around the drive and drove off very slowly, though he probably wanted to toss a few pieces of gravel. It was that kind of day.

Inside I stirred up the wood burning stove and then tossed in some fresh cedar. I grabbed a blanket and wrapped it around me Indian style and sat on the couch. I was already staring at Des's book when Melanie came in with two glasses and a bottle of red wine. I knew she would not be drinking because of the baby, but the gesture sweet.

"Girl talk?" She knew her little sister.

"Get in here, Doc, and pour out some of that medicine."

A minute later we were sharing the blanket as I sampled the wine.

"I wish you didn't dislike Des so much, Mel. You really don't even know him."

"He made a bad first impression on me."

"I know."

"Look, he was married and messing around with my little sister."

"But, your sister was messing around with him, too."

Melanie is beautiful even when she frowns. I was getting a good one right then.

"Oh shit, you're right," she said still frowning, but backing off a bit. "If you two are happy with your...whatever it is you have, then I am okay, too. But, something tells me it is not all peaches and cream between you guys. I saw more warmth between you before he got divorced. So, like, what is it, Sony?"

It was a pretty good red wine. I let a swallow ease down into my tummy while I gathered my thoughts. I wasn't sure I liked the ripples in the fountain of truth that followed.

"Maybe...maybe it was better when he was unavailable."

Mel set her glass down and nodded. She waited patiently for me to go on.

"Mel, Des and I used to be hot news. We once were an international scandal. The star-crossed poets on an adulterous spree through Europe. People following us with cameras. Tabloid stories that accented anything remotely lurid."

"I remember."

"Hah, that's it you remember. It's all gone now!"

"And you miss that?"

"Maybe. But, Mel it was all a lie. The real story of what went on between Des and me is pretty tame. We fell in love with each other's poetry. It was like we were the only two aliens living on another planet. Nobody else understood us. We let it go too far one night in Ireland and a myth was born. We held hands and I wore his necklace. Then we allowed it to be blown out of proportion because it was our inside joke. It sold our books. Our tabloid couple name was 'Desony'. So freakin' cute."

"So you rode the wave."

"We did. I was the pretty little kidnapped girl who escaped African bandits only to be captured by an Irish gigolo. So funny I could cry."

"Okay, sis, I knew all of that. But, what is it now? Why is he here? Why are you two still hanging on? If it's not love then what?"

I knew Mel would get down to it sooner or later.

"I don't know, Mel."

There was a knock on the door as Ray came in holding Mel's cell phone.

"Sorry to intrude, but its Dr. Reed from Caduses, Mel."

"Yeah, okay, I've been waiting for that call," said Mel. She got up and took the phone with her out the door leaving me and Ray. It was a handoff.

"Come on in, Ray. How's the forgotten man doing?"

He came in and sat down next to me, a wry smile on his handsome face.

"The forgotten man?"

"That's what Bim called you."

"I'll have to think about that."

"I think he was referring to all the attention Melanie is getting about the baby."

"Well, I expected that."

"You cool with being here and all that?"

"Yeah, I am. Mel and I needed some time together. God knows we have had this career driven marriage."

"So you knocked her up so you could be together. Very nice move."

"I like your moves, too, kid. With Des up in the Bollander house and all."

"Definitely not what you think."

"Then what is it?"

Ray had picked up where his wife had left off with the big money question, but the moment was gone. When I went silent he knew it, too.

"Okay, Sony, I'll leave you alone." He started to head for the door.

"Sorry, okay. It's been a weird day. I want to talk to you more. I won't let you be forgotten, Ray."

"Gotcha. I gotta go in and make sure she doesn't take off and have the baby in Nepal or someplace."

I smiled and waved him out the door. When he left my eyes immediately went to the manuscript. I think it was time to find out what Des was up to. I finished it about three hours later. I don't think I will ever be the same again. The book was flawless. I never thought I would ever read something in Roland's class, but I just had. Oh shit!

CHAPTER THIRTY

MOLLY

Taos. Okay, not the ideal choice for a November honeymoon, but it fit into our plans. Owen had already been scheduled to speak at a veterinary seminar there so our airfare and rooms were paid for. It is also an awesome place to Christmas shop and the scenery is breathtaking. Of course, day one was mostly spent on the phone talking to Pat and the girls about Bim's condition. It seems he is going to be okay. I was so glad Dr. Melanie and Dr. Palmer were both in attendance at Yalanek's to make sure Bim was going to make it out of there. He just went down like a felled tree. It was so sweet when he told me how sorry he was to ruin our wedding day. He also told me as the EMT's were taking him out that he had something very important to tell me. I wanted to ask what, but they were moving him. Guess I will have to wait until I get home to find that part out.

My husband, Owen (I like the sound of that) and I had quite a bit of free time to wander around the small village. He had one lecture to give on the evening of our second day and the rest of the time was pretty much our own. His topic was 'The Migrations of *Puma concolor* Into Population Centers and Their Effect on Domestic Animals'. In other words, cougars in your backyard. When he spoke on this topic, colleagues tended to listen very carefully.

On our third day in Taos we were out shopping. It had snowed just slightly overnight and now the bright sun was reflecting off the peaks surrounding the town. It was one of those days where everything is so colorful and beautiful to the eye that it seems like you are walking within a postcard. Taos, of course, is an artist colony and we had already purchased some gorgeous pottery for gifts. I also found necklaces, earrings, and bracelets, but hadn't decided who would get what yet. Owen bought a rug for his office and we decided since we had to ship that home, we would ship everything else along with it. I was having a ball and so was my husband. Still love that word.

As the setting sun was banking off of the Sangre de Christo Mountains, turning them deep gold, we ducked into one last art gallery before heading back to the hotel for dinner. It was not a big salon, but very charming with pinon pine columns and moody lighting. A pretty girl handed us glasses of white wine to sip while we browsed. I found myself checking out the price tags before I looked at the paintings. They were all very high priced works of art, but my God, were they lovely.

I found myself standing in front of one painting that seemed to capture the view of the mountains that we had just left outside.

"Honey, take a look at this one." Owen drifted over.

"Wow, that is gorgeous. How much?"

I squinted at the card and saw the price. "Whoa, too much. $3450."

I looked at Owen and he was rolling his eyes and doing a silent whistle.

"Who's the artist, Mol?"

"Well", I said, looking back at the card. "It's says...oh my God!"

Owen leaned over my shoulder.

"Meg Bollander!" I almost shouted I was so surprised. I was not aware that a woman had walked up behind us until she spoke.

"She's quite the artist, isn't she?" said the woman. "And it's a small world, isn't it, Molly Costello?"

It took me a minute to recognize Leah Harrison. We had not known each other for long years ago, but she had shared some history with our family.

"Leah?"

"Good memory, Molly. Hello, welcome to my Taos gallery," she said. She nodded to Owen. He didn't know her at all, but was enjoying my surprise.

"I am not surprised that you gravitated to Meg's painting," Leah said.

"I had no idea it was hers, but then the book I have on my coffee table at home is all paintings of Lake Winnebago. She has branched out."

"I had Meg here last year to work. As you can see she put a lot of thought and love into this canvas."

"She's not still here, is she?" My eyes darted around as if I expected to see Meg pop up next.

"No she's back in California with her sister. Meg's slipping a little lately I'm afraid. She's still full of piss and vinegar, but doling it out in smaller doses these days."

"And Karin?" Karin was Roland Heinz's wife at one time. We had bonded when she came back to Wisconsin to reconcile with her sister, Meg. Leah was the sister of Karin's second husband. Yeah, it's complicated. Leah made a gesture to the wine girl to bring us another glass and then led us into her office. We sat on a couch beneath another Bollander painting of the Taos Pueblo.

"Karin is very well. This meeting will tickle her." Leah paused. "So, Molly, how are you all doing?" She was looking at Owen.

"Oh, my, sorry Leah this is my husband, Owen Palmer." I was so surprised that I had forgotten to introduce them. "Actually, we are here on our honeymoon."

"Well, congratulations to you both. She turned to me and whispered, "Is this the veterinarian?"

It would have been a little embarrassing if it wasn't. "You have a good memory, too. Yep, the same guy."

I could see she was doing some calculating about how long our engagement had lasted. It produced a smile that said she didn't really need to know the whole story.

"And your girls? How are they? I, of course, have followed Sonia's adventures a little."

"Yes, adventures. That's putting it mildly." Very mildly. "They are both fine. Sony is home with us for a while doing some writing and Melanie and her husband are staying with us until she has her baby in January."

"Oh, how wonderful. I assume you still live in the same place?"

"Oh yeah, we wouldn't leave Roland's Ghost Farm for anything. Owen has his vet clinic in the barn now, too."

"And what about Meg's old place? Is it still standing?"

I looked at Owen knowingly before I spoke. "Yes, it is still there. In fact, someone we know is renting it."

"Oh?"

"He's another poet. One of Sonia's friends." That sounded so over-simplified that I almost choked on the words. "Did you know that the house was untouched since she moved out? No one had ever cleaned it up or anything. Wasn't there anything there that Meg wanted?"

"I doubt it. She made a pretty clean break. I do know that house was listed for years with no takers. They said it was too much of a fixer-upper. I think it was bought by a bank back there and they probably sold it to a realtor for a rental. It was a dump ten years ago; I can only imagine what it is like today."

"Well, tell her that at least the place is still inspiring some-one. It seems our poet friend has written quite a bit up there."

"I will tell her."

Owen and I exchanged the 'we'd better be going look' and Leah picked it up.

"I'm sure you honeymooners have plans. I am so glad you came in here today, Molly."

"Oh, me, too."

"And you're sure you're not interested in the Bollander oil out front? You get the family discount, you know?" She slid a card to Owen.

"We'll think it over, Leah," I said.

"Okay," she said and stood. We all stood. "Give my best to the girls and again, congratulations on the marriage."

"I will and thanks. My love to Meg and Karin."

"Can you ship the painting to Pipe?" Owen said, which made me stop in my tracks.

"I can ship it anywhere," said Leah with a nod and a smile.

I looked at Owen. He was serious.

"I'll be by tomorrow with a check," he said. I was in shock as we said adios to Leah.

Back out on the street I was finally able to speak. "What did you just do?"

"I just bought you a wedding gift."

"Oh, honey."

"Listen, Molly, no postcard, photo, or sketch could ever capture our honeymoon the way that painting did. Look." He pointed at the last of the sun at the very tips of the mountain peaks. "Meg had seen that color and somehow recreated it. In a way, the painting would be like our rings: reminders of our pasts and promises, now forever linked."

We skipped dinner that night…and breakfast the next morning.

At the Albuquerque Airport I spent most of the time on the phone again. Things had quieted down back home on most fronts, but I could tell when I talked to Sony that something was wrong with her. I knew it had to have something to do with 'our poet friend,' but she wouldn't get into it. I knew she was going to read his book so I asked her how it was. Big mistake. I had inadvertently hit on her sore spot. As a novelist myself, I was now very curious about his book. I already knew from someone at Stompe that they were going to publish it. There was a rumor that it was a pretty amazing book. So why was my daughter so upset with it? Maybe there was something personal in the story that had her vexed. All I knew was I wanted to read it as soon as I got home. If Des had betrayed Sony in some way in his book then he had just had his last strike with me.

"You look pissed." Own said just before we were to board our plane. "Something wrong back home?"

"It's Sonia."

"You mean Sonia and Des, right?"

I nodded. "There's something in his new book that she doesn't like."

"Any clues?"

"Nada. But, all of that can wait. I want to enjoy the last minutes of our honeymoon. This was kind of perfect, wasn't it?"

"Well, we didn't get tans."

"My skin feels tanned, sweetie."

"Mine, too, Sunshine."

CHAPTER THIRTY-ONE

DESMOND

The walking man, the expatriate bleak of eye was on and about a quest. He sought out a graveyard perhaps lost forever among the fields and farms, whose silos where like steeples full of hay above church pews filled by cows giving milk and manure back to the land. The man had a map in one hand and his heart in t'other. He was looking for the mum and da of his da. Grandfolks. Good folks, who had fled the Potato Famine to find a Holyland over and around the curve of the earth in a time so hard that everything broke in two that was tossed against it. The pie-faced boy, who was his da, was sent home after the barn fire, back to Eire as an orphan boy. When this walking man was a lad that father-come-home told him about a great inland sea like Galilee in the Bible and soil so fertile it could grow green a new Eden. He told him that his grandfolks lay in a ring of stone near a town called St. Anne and that the Amish would know where that might be. The walking man had a map in one hand and his heart in t'other.

And so begins my novel, *Above Galilee.* It must have been waiting to be written by someone who would sit in that chair and look out at that view of Winnebago. The fact that it was Desmond O'Conner is still a mystery to me. The book was whispered in my ear and I typed it more like a dictation that a creation. I had felt the magical quality of the Bollander house as soon as I stepped into it. That was why I dared not touch a thing; not move so much as dirty glass or a cricket corpse. There was a spell cast and I was afraid my very presence might disturb it and send it away. It was only later that I realized it was waiting for me. Hah, the Costellos think they have ghosts down at their farm. They all should spend a night up here on The Ledge.

I find it rather interesting that Stompe Publishing loves my book and Sonia Costello seems to hate it. I expected at least a polite review from her, but her continued silence leads me to believe she thinks its horse crap. I suppose these things are subjective, but because of our relationship (or whatever it is) I thought we would at least have a literary conversation about it. Like a chess player, I sit up here stumped as to my next move on the board. How can I break this silence between us? She won't return my calls and I can't just drop in down there with her sister ready to take a broom to me. My head was splitting when my agent called. The chirp of the mobile phone made me jump.

"Hello, Cedric."

"Good day, Des. Is that disappointment I hear in your voice?"

"Only so far as I had hoped it was someone else."

"Of course. Well, 'tis I."

"'Tis."

"Okay, I cannot deal with your moods over the phone so I will state my business and ring off."

I was not in the mood for his snit voice. We did this dance often enough. Besides, my career was looking up again. I felt more in control of my agent that I did a couple months ago when he was calling the shots. I chose to be paternally kind.

"I apologize, Ced. I am having a wee bit of trouble with the lady. I should not let it spill over on you. Sorry, man."

There was silence for a couple beats.

"I must have the bloody wrong number. An apology from Desmond O'Conner?"

"Hold the sarcasm. I am trying to be nice to you. I am not feeling up to our usual sparring today."

"Well, then I am sorry, too. We could have a kiss and hug if you were here."

"You'd like that." Now I was smiling.

"Okay, let's move on. Des, I have emailed you the details of your book deal. I think it is generous and you should sign the papers when you get them. The editors are already at it."

"Before I even sign?"

"I told them to go ahead."

So much for my illusion of control. But, then I had come to trust Cedric.

"What else?" I asked.

"Someone is going to call you about a cover concept. Got any?"

"Maybe."

"Good. Now I assume you would like to know about your advance?"

"Of course."

"Well, because of the quality of writing, your international name recognition, and your semi-connection to Roland Heinz…"

I had to think about that last part.

"…I got you $125, 000 dollars."

I had not expected that much of an advance. I knew the damned book was good. I would not have submitted it if it wasn't. I also knew Stompe had calculated sales so apparently they were making it a top priority book. I was back and I was back as a novelist.

"That is quite generous of them." My voice cracked a bit. "Did you get the check yet?"

"Oh yes, I didn't want to call until I got the money deposited. Not a check, but rather a wire transfer. In case you didn't know, no one writes checks anymore."

He was being supercilious again, but I didn't care. The man was definitely a book agent now.

"What's your cut these days, if I may ask?"

"Eight per cent. If you wish to throw in a bonus…"

"I'll throw you a bonus."

"Yes, well, what else can I do for you today, boss?"

"Actually, I have a project for you, Ced."

"Which is?"

"Work your magic and buy this house."

"That would be the house there…in Pipe, is it?"

"That would be the one. You already have the realtor's information. Buy the property as fast as you can do it."

"You told me it is a tumbledown wreck."

"Soon to be my wreck."

"You want to spend your advance on an old farm house, correct?"

"Yes! Call me back when the deal is done. And it won't be a lot of money either. I know they have given up selling this place. Make their day. Make mine."

"As you wish. I will need to also collect a realty commission from you and…"

I hung up on Cedric. There was no other way to get him off of me and onto his next task. A second later I got a text message from him: "fuk u" Perfect.

The Bollander place became the O'Conner place about four days later. The realtor brought out a bottle of champagne along with the paperwork. I knew the locals would always think of it as Meg Bollander's house so we toasted her in her living room amid all of her clutter. I still had no intention of ever changing a thing in the house. The house and I would age and die together, I thought. You see, what I found in that house I could never find in any other place on earth; whether it be a palace or a shack. I found my true writer's ear here. The whisper. With or without my beloved Sonia, I was now bound to The Ledge with The Holyland for me backyard.

CHAPTER THIRTY-ONE

SONIA

There was a pleasant buzz going around me here at Ghost Farm. Mom and Owen were back home and going about decorating the place for Christmas. Mel and Ray were buying baby clothes and a crib was now waiting in the corner of our old bedroom. I should mention that they already know that they are having a boy. I heard them kicking around names and Ray the Third is at the top of the list.

In town, Pat and Bim are both doing well now. Pat is looking much better and Bim, though he seems to have shrunk a little, is back in the garage. Carrie is out here almost every day doing things with Mom and Mel. Mike is off on a photo shoot in Chicago, but he'll be back in a couple days and staying until Christmas. And me? Well, I am mostly hiding out in the cheese shed like a round of cheddar, aging and getting stinky.

I guess it is time to explain my behavior. Yes, it all has to do with Des' book. I read it. In fact, I have read it three times now. It is an amazing piece of work. Nothing I have ever read comes as close to Roland's writing as this book. So why had it rocked my world so much? Well, this is sounding very petty to me as I type it out, but the book has created a chasm between me and Des that I feel is now unbridgeable. Where we were once on the same road, he has now taken a diverging pathway and has moved away and light years ahead of me. Okay, I need to explain this.

When we met, I was the superstar. I was well known and successful. I was the target of the press and cameras. I, I, I. Me, me, me. Des treated me like a princess. When we got close and began to share our poetry, mine was head and shoulders above his. He knew it and told me over and over how much better my ear was for words. People at Stompe told me the same things. Critics loved my work and he was generally regarded as a fading star. He had his day and it was gone. My potential was limitless.

So you read that last paragraph and you think what a conceited little bitch I am. And you'd be absolutely right. Only now I am not that person. It kills me to not be her, but I should have realized last summer when Sarah Dylan upstaged me that I was getting stale. I kind of realized that for a while actually, until Des told me about pushing her away for me. I took his affection for me and tied it back to my supposed talent. Well, his book slammed me back to reality. Nothing I had ever written or will ever write can compete with his work from now on. Good for him, sad for me. Sad for us because I find I cannot face him. I need some help, but don't know where to turn.

And then today, the news comes that he has bought Meg's house. It seems he will be living right above me forever; as constant a reminder of my problem as it was for Roland to know Meg was up there. Only there is no loathing between us. I do fear we are going to share a lost love, though. I need to move away, but I can't do anything until the holidays are over and Melanie has her baby. After that, I will leave. Maybe go back to Nairobi and get active in running my school. If someone wants to shoot me, well I could wear a bull's eye t-shirt. God, I am miserable, aren't I?

I was in town doing some Christmas shopping when I drove by the Stouffer's. I slowed down to see if Bim was in the garage. Duh, of course he was. It was twenty degrees out and the weatherman was calling for a big snow storm to roll in overnight, but nothing kept Bim indoors. I parked in front of the house and headed up the driveway. Of all the people I know, the garage sitter was my confessor and advisor of choice. Bim Stouffer was my Yoda. He was starting to look like Yoda now, too.

"Well, hello little girl," he said. I noticed his voice was a little strained and slurry. Not too bad, but I could hear the effects of the last stroke. He was bundled up in an old orange hunting suit with a space heater humming beside him.

"Hi, Bim. May the force be with you."

"Huh?"

"Nothing it's a line from an old movie. You look like one of the characters."

"I'll bet I do. What brings you out today, Sony?"

I sat down in the lawn chair next to Bim's wheelchair and closest to the space heater. It was actually not too bad in the garage and out of the wind.

"I got the blues, Bim."

"Jah, I can tell that. Want a beer?"

"Are you supposed to be drinking beer after your…you know?"

"Yeah I know and the answer is who cares. You got the blues and I'm stuck in a wheelchair. You want a beer?"

"Sure."

"In the cooler."

I opened the little cooler and took out a beer. "Still drinking the cheap stuff, huh?"

"Beer is beer."

"I suppose." I cracked open the can and took a gulp. "Tastes good."

"Should. Beer is good for you."

"Remember when I used to scold you about drinking out here in the morning?"

"I remember. Times change, eh?"

I sighed. "They sure do."

"So what's got you down? Not that Irishman, I hope."

I gave Bim a look that confirmed his fear.

"What has that bastard done to you now, girl?"

"He wrote a book."

That gave even the great Bimster pause. He opened his mouth and then shut it. I hope I hadn't caused a short circuit.

"Let me get this straight," he finally said, "a writer writes a book and it has you moping around and sighing?"

"Sounds stupid, eh?"

"You'd better fill me in."

At that moment Mom's car pulled into the driveway. I didn't know if it was because she saw my car out front or if she was just visiting Pat. An old instinct told me to quick hide my beer. It was too late.

"So you two are drinkin' in the garage already today." she said with a knowing smile. It was no surprise what Bim was doing, but I amused her.

"We're just having a little chat Mrs. Palmer. Noticed I dropped the Miss Perfect?"

"I noticed, but I am still Molly Costello, Bim. It's my professional name."

"What no hyphens?" Bim asked.

"I'll think about the hyphen." She said.

"Have a seat Molly. I've been wanting to have talk to both of you and now the chance has popped up unexpected. Pat and Carrie are at the damned mall so we are alone."

Mom scooted another lawn chair up as I handed her a beer. She looked at the can and then me and shrugged. Almost at the same moment a large crow landed in the driveway. It caught all our attention. It was satin black and it cocked its head, locking intelligent eyes on us. It strutted right up to within a few feet of where we all sat and let out a loud 'caw'.

"Cocky fellow, isn't he?" said Mom.

"Looking for food," I added.

"Hah," said Bim, "the messenger bird has come to make sure I get my story straight."

Mom got a weird look on her face. "You called it a messenger bird?"

"Sure, Roland wrote a lot about messenger birds, remember?"

"I sure do now," said Mom. After a pensive moment on her part she asked, "what do you need to talk to both of us about, Bim?"

"Well girls, as a matter of fact I want to talk to you about Roland."

The crow flew away. I suppose its mission was accomplished.

"Okaaaay," Mom said making that word long and drawn out.

"And Des O'Conner, too," Bim added.

"Huh? I murmured. I didn't expect that add on. I noticed that it had started to snow very lightly even though the sun was trying to come out. Mom and I had our beer and our seats. Bim definitely had our attention.

CHAPTER THIRTY-TWO

BIM

I finally had Sony and Molly in a time a place to reveal some secrets to them. It was stuff they probably needed to know. I knew Molly and Sony were both down on Des and while most of it was none of my business, some of it was.

I began: "It was a day just like this one almost, maybe fifteen years ago or so, that Roland walked up the driveway two doors down from here. A bitter cold January day in the last week of his life. My wife had just passed and I hadn't seen him for quite a while, but I had heard he was not doing well. I was surprised to see him, but I didn't let on.

"Hello, Roland, what are you up to?"

"About six two, Bim. Still sitting in the garage, eh?"

"It's my living room," I said and handed him a beer.

I saw Molly and Sonia smile.

I continued: "Roland took the beer and took a chair."

"I suppose you're wondering what brings me over today, Bim?"

"Well, it's been a while, Rollie. I guess our circles just don't cross as much as they used to."

He thought about that. "I was sorry to hear about your wife. I wanted to get to Stanhope's for the wake, but I was having a bad day."

"So you've come by to pay your respects. Thanks, Rollie."

"Well, that and more."

I could tell now that my old friend Roland Heinz was a short timer. He had that look. His eyes, usually clear as a hawk's were now rheumy and without light. I gave him his time to gather his thoughts. I knew he had stopped by for something more than late condolences for a wife he knew I didn't particularly grieve over.

"You and I go way back, Bim. Lots of common water passed under our bridges."

"True. Lots of whiskey and beer, too."

"Yeah, the bad old days, eh? Well, those days catch up with all of us. My health is failing now, but no regrets about those days. Not a one."

He paused. "Well, maybe a few."

I read his mind. He was thinking about the Bollander sisters.

He continued: "Bim, I'm dying. And don't look at me like that. It's just a fact of life. Another fact is I am in need of a friend to take care of some business before I go and you are the one who jumped right into my mind."

If anyone but Roland had come to me with a deathbed request I would have hedged. Not him. Only him. "Ask me anything, Rollie."

"Listen to me carefully. I don't want to have to say it over. I simply don't have the time. You are going to find out in a few days that I have adopted a young woman to be my daughter. She has two little kids herself, who will be my grandchildren."

I would have been astounded, but this was Roland Heinz.

"Who, Rollie?"

"No one you know. They are not from around here. Listen, Bim, don't ask any hard questions. This is a done deal. Something I wanted and planned for a while."

"So what's my part in this?"

"I'm getting to that, okay? I am leaving them everything I have, the farm, the estate, the whole ball of wax."

"Whew," I whistled. I figured that was a fair fortune since Rollie had won those prizes and become world famous. Of course, almost nobody around town knew that. The only rich people we knew were the ones who won the Powerball. "That's a lot of cashola."

"Well, yes it is. But, I still need you to handle something for me."

With that statement he produced a manila envelope. It was sealed with scotch tape and my name was on the outside. He handed it to me. I waited for his explanation.

I could see Molly and Sony literally lean into me. It was a good story so far.

"In this envelope is the code number to a bank account. It's in Switzerland."

"No shit!" I had always heard about Swiss bank accounts and now I was holding one.

"Yeah, well, I have a trust to place in you, Bim. After I'm gone,..."

He sort of swallowed hard as he spoke. I knew this was hard for him.

"After I'm gone those girls are going to be on their own. Yes, I am leaving them enough money to be very comfortable, but I am not sure if they will stay around here or go back to their lives back East. Either way, I figured they might need some sort of insurance. A little stash for a rainy day. You know Harry Stompe, right?"

"Of course," I said. Harry was Roland's old friend and we had met several times over the years. I hadn't seen or heard from him in ages. I knew he was Roland's publisher now, too.

"Harry will always keep his eye on my family, but he isn't getting any younger either. I need a back up and that would be you"

"I think I see. I am a safety net. But, why not just give them this money now?"

"I could, but there is no emergency now. I have found that hard rains fall when you least expect them. There are twists and turns that you just can't plan for. Those days are what fathers and grandfathers are for. Only I won't be around. You will, Bim. Do you understand?"

Well, I got it. I was overwhelmed with the trust Roland put in me. It seemed to raise me up. I hadn't contemplated much beyond the garage back then. I agreed to all his conditions.

Roland got up and started to leave, but he had a parting thought.

"Didn't you always have a thing for that lady next door?"

"Two doors down. She lives two houses down. Why?"

"She a widow, right?"

"Yeah."

"Well, you want to sit in your garage alone forever?"

To Molly and Sonia: "Those were his last words to me. I never saw Roland Heinz again. The deal was if my health was getting bad and Harry was gone I was to give the balance of Roland's rainy day money to you. I kept that envelope stashed in a cedar chest in our bedroom all this time."

"I see," said Molly. "And now you think you should tell us about this bank account and turn it over to us? Bim, I appreciate the role you have been playing all these years, but you are not dying yet and..."

"Molly, shut up. I could flop over like a flounder any second. That's why I'm telling you all this stuff."

"Bim," said Sony looking at her mom. "We really don't need that money anymore. Right, Mom? Why don't you and Pat just keep it?"

"Yes," said Molly jumping in. "Leave it for Pat and your great grandchild."

"Well, that's a nice thought, girls, but the fact is the money I have told you about it already spent."

Ah, now I see confusion spreading across their faces. The money, though now un-needed by them, has been embezzled by the garage sitter. But, why would he tell them this story if he wiped out the mysterious Swiss bank account? Why indeed? Maybe I was enjoying this tale a little too much. It was far from over.

"Have another beer, girls, and listen. You might need it for the rest of this story. They both took another beer like they wouldn't get the ending without it.

"One day out of nowhere I get a phone call. Pat comes out and says some man with an Irish accent is on the phone in the house. I figured it was someone calling to try to sell me an Irish Sweepstakes ticket. Well, it was Desmond O'Conner."

Now both of their expressions had gone to stupid. Especially Sonia. I decided to put them both out of their misery and quickly finished the story. A dead six pack of cans lay on the garage floor as they both drove off. I felt unburdened and somehow happy. No more secrets to keep. Today, the messenger bird was an old coot.

CHAPTER THIRTY-THREE

DESMOND

I heard that rattle of gravel in the drive announcing a visitor. I had just checked out the weather on my computer and I was trying to think what I needed to do to prepare for a snowstorm. I had a little food, a little booze, and tons of time. Now I also had Sony and Molly getting out of a car and heading for my door. They didn't appear to be armed so I figured I was slightly ahead of the game. I met them on the back stoop.

"I didn't expect to see you two come 'a calling."

"Well, here we are," said Sony.

There was something afoot. Both women had strange expressions. I could tell they had something important to say, but I had no idea what. Unless...

"Can we come in?" Molly asked as she went by me into the kitchen followed by Sony.

"Of course," I said. I paused a moment before following them and looked up at the sky out over the lake. I could see a couple pockets of blue ahead of a deep purple wall of clouds. The wind had gone dead calm and the oak tree in the yard was filled with starlings hunkering down. I could smell the coming snow.

Inside the Costello's were already sitting on my battered couch. They had not removed their coats. All that was needed was me to sit in my easy chair throne, which I did.

"Tea?" I asked politely.

"No thanks," said Sony. "It's gonna snow soon so we won't be here for long."

"Oh, okay." I looked at both of them wondering who was going to tell me why they were here. Molly began.

"We just had the most amazing talk with Bim Stouffer."

I got it now. Bim knew I would need to come clean sooner or later. Apparently, he had decided to give me a shove. "I see."

"Des, we know most of it. I just want your side of the story. Then we might have a little Q and A session," said Sony.

"Bim told you about our association?"

They both nodded. I took a deep breath. I really wanted a drink for a prop, but I just figured I would get it all out and be done with it. I wasn't sure what the upshots would be, but what he hell.

"Okay, as you know this Ali Halloran character and I were students and friends at Trinity many years ago. We shared a love of literature and poetry, but we mostly bonded over a class we took on the works of your famous Papa, Roland Heinz. That picture that you showed me was probably taken during one of our pub discussions about Garnet Granger and her dreams. We would talk about those books and would write poems about them on pub napkins and coasters. Well, as time went by he and I drifted apart as college mates do. The only thing I knew about what happened to him was when I ran into his mum at the market one day. She said he was in England and doing something with the government. I remember that struck me as odd. He hated the Brits, I thought, especially anything to do with the Royals and their government. I quickly forgot about Ali and never heard a word about him again. Until…"

I paused to make sure my audience was not ahead or behind me. They were all ears, as they say. I cleared my throat and continued.

"Well, as you know, a few years later I had made a little name for myself thanks to Harry Stompe. I had met you, Molly, at one of his parties in fact. But, I still didn't know you, Sony. You were about to become famous, though I wouldn't hear about it right off. I rarely watched the news or read the papers back then. Then one day I got a call from my old friend, Ali.

"Well, I was surprised to hear from him and wondered why he had rung me up. I asked him what he'd been up to. I thought I would get some sort of banal sketch of his life, but instead I got…well, involved in it."

Sony and Molly nodded as if to urge me to talk faster. I am Irish and this sort of storytelling has its own pace.

"Ali quickly told me to shut up and listen to him. He said time was of the essence. He said he was in Africa doing a little job and had run into a problem. He was vague about what his line of work was. In fact, he cut me off when I asked. He asked me if I had heard about an American girl who had been kidnapped in the Sudan. I told him that maybe I had heard something about it and why did he ask. That phone call suddenly took a murky turn.

"He asked me if I knew that Roland Heinz had a granddaughter. I remembered that he had adopted a family. Ali, told me that Darfur bandits had snatched the granddaughter and were holding her for ransom. I was horrified because I knew that those things usually ended badly, especially for women. I asked him what it had to do with me. Ali told me he had some 'loose ties' to this bandit group, which shocked me. He said he was involved with the negotiations for the ransom. Finally, rounding about to me he asked me, since I was published by Stompe, if I knew anyone in the Heinz camp."

"I never heard it put that way," said Molly.

"Yes, well, I was not in the Heinz camp at the time and would have loved to hang up on this business, but Ali was insistent. He said if I knew anyone to contact that he and I owed it to Roland to follow through and save his kin. All I could only lamely offer was that I had met you, Molly, once at a party.

"He asked if I had a phone number. I found your card in my wallet, Molly, and there was a phone number on it. I took a deep breath and gave it to him."

"That was the first call to the farm from the kidnapper. The FBI was already involved and taping calls," Molly said. "I remember writing down a contact number, the rest is a blur."

"Well, Ali knew, of course, that they were listening. There was some operation going on over there that he was involved in that was in danger if too much information got out to authorities over here in the US.

"Listen, what no one knew was that Ali worked for British Intelligence. It seems they recruited Arab-Anglos for under-cover work around the world. I guess Ali was their man in Dar-fur. That is all Ali could tell me. I think he was trying to win my confidence. I was dubious, but it made sense later. As it turned out, I couldn't do much of anything to help you, Sony. Or at least that is what I thought."

I could see the ladies were putting the two stories together. Light bulbs were coming on in their brains.

"Okay, Bim skipped the part about how he managed to contact Ali. What happened, Des?" asked Sony.

"Well, you know now that old Bim was assigned by Roland to be your guardian angel in case of an emergency, right? Well, your kidnapping qualified as such. When it became apparent that the FBI was stalling he took action. He didn't even bother to consult with Harry Stompe."

"The FBI told us not to pay right away," Molly said. "They said they needed some sort of assurances. Locations. Local contacts. Harry and I had the money, but we were being advised to wait until some sort of an operation could be set up. They…" She looked at Sony. "They said you would most likely be killed as soon as the ransom was paid if you were not dead already."

Sonia looked down and nodded.

"Bim and Pat," I continued, "were over at your house one night during all of this, right? He did some snooping and found the contact number, which was in a prominent place next to your house phone in the living room. He copied the number and when he got home, he placed a call to Ali. Ali rang me back and asked me to follow up with Bim. He knew I could ask the right questions about his relationship to the Costellos. I cleared Bim and Ali asked me to set it all up. I placed a call to Bim and he told me he had the money and could have it wired anywhere in the world within the hour. What no one knew was that Ali had some sway with the bandits because they believed he was Al Qaeda in the Sudan. He was revered and feared by those men. That is how he controlled them and kept you alive, Sony."

"I remember that he told me that he was not who he seemed to be."

"Indeed, he wasn't, thank God," I said. As I said, Bim transferred the money into Ali's hands. In the short version, he paid off the bandits and got you to the border."

"And the long version?" asked Molly.

"The long version is that Ali screwed them. It cost half of the ransom money in bribes just to get you out of Africa. He was so deep under cover that no one else could help him. Unfortunately, there are few secrets in that part of the world, too many crossed ties. The bandits' head man found out he had been stiffed. You were gone, but this guy, whose name was Ovid D'uon swore an oath to avenge the betrayal. And since he could never find Ali again, when the opportunity arose to kill you, Sony…"

"Holy shit! I was a sitting duck in Nairobi. It was well publicized that the school was my project."

"Exactly. Someone should have warned you, but you were everywhere in those days."

"I wouldn't have listened anyway. I was too freaking famous."

"Honey, don't…" Molly said when Sony began to cry.

"I assume Bim showed you the photo of the burned van in Nairobi?"

"Yes, he said it was closure."

"The body of the man found in that charred wreck was confirmed as that of Ovid D'uon. No doubt about it. We all have to assume that with Ali's contacts that he is telling us the facts. When he called me with the news of this guy's death he swore on 'the books of Roland.' I think that oath binds us all. It's all over."

"So your only part in all of this was giving your friend Mom's phone number?" Sony asked.

"Yes, that and telling Bim where to send the ransom. I learned the rest of the story later. I always thought it would complicate our relationship if you knew about my involvement. I was trying to think of a good time to tell you the rest of this, but you disappeared on me. Why, Sony?"

Molly, good mother that she is, realized that the rest of this conversation was private. She stood and made her exit. Sonia and I were left alone in a house soon to be buried in snow.

CHAPTER THIRTY-FOUR

SONIA

I watched the snowflakes begin to fall through the widow that faced the lake. Des was in the kitchen trying to find a corkscrew to open an old wine bottle. I refused to drink the other stuff that Meg left laying around and I never did acquire a taste for Irish whiskey. I had stayed behind because Des and I had things to talk over. Lots of them. But, the snow was doing strange things to my mind. It was starting a war between the poet in me and the person who had pouted about Des' book for a couple weeks. I looked around and wondered if there were more snowflakes outside than dust motes in the old house. The storm clouds had closed off the sky and only fading gray light lit the room. I heard the sound of a cork being released and soon Des was handing me a glass of red.

"What is it?" I asked as I sniffed the wine.

"It's a charming little domestic merlot. Well aged, I'd say. Probably been in the wine cellar under the sink for a couple decades. I couldn't quite read the label as the mice seemed to have consumed it."

"Lovely." I took a tentative sip.

"Vinegar?"

"Not quite. Sit down, Des, you're hovering."

"Sorry."

He nestled into his chair. I saw his laptop on the floor beside him and tried to picture him writing there day and night. The gloom in the room was palpable, but yet there was some edgy vibe in the air. I don't mean between us either. It was more like a creative current. I had the thought that I could maybe write in that chair, too. In fact, I thought I might want to give it a try someday. Not now. I sipped the wine and found it bitter, but okay to swallow.

"You wrote that book sitting right there?"

"I did. That book that you never read."

"Actually, I did read it."

Des looked surprised. He cocked his head like a dog. "You read it and had nothing to say?"

"Not until now." I mimicked his head cocking.

Des had a jelly jar of whiskey and sipped it. "What, may I ask, did you think of it?"

This scenario was a tad stiff considering everything that had gone on between us. I shook my head and almost wanted to cry again. Why was a book review so emotional?

"The book…your novel is wonderful."

"That's a good start."

"And I hate you for it."

He set down his jar. "Not so good."

"Oh, Des, it's a beautiful book. It's Rolandesque. I was crying and laughing through every page. When I was done all I could selfishly think about was how you had passed me as a writer at the speed of light. It wasn't just jealousy either, it was fear.'

"Fear? Jaysus, Sony. I wrote the thing for you."

That statement threw me. I could only shake my head again. Des had become only a shadow now as the room was growing darker. Only the glow of the yard light off the new snow was providing a shadowless hint of vision.

"I thought of you and our trip into the Holylands. I found a title and typed it and then something happened. Do you believe in ghosts?"

I nodded slowly like a child around a campfire. Ghosts were as real as us Costello's at our farm.

"The book was whispered to me."

"Roland?"

He shook his head.

"Meg Bollander?"

Again a head shake.

"T'was your voice in me ear, girl. T'was a tale told by your lips."

"T'was?" I got a chill and the hair stood up on the back of my neck and arms.

"Yes."

I was trying to figure this out and took another sip of wine. "This sounds a bit like your Blarney."

"Hah! Blarney, is it?"

"Yeah, when you slip into that accent."

"Well, here's the Blarney of it. Think about it; every thing you write comes from a voice inside of you. Did you ever stop to ask yourself who was telling you your poems? Whose voice did they come to you in? Think."

"I never thought about it."

"An honest answer. But, I did think about it. Me gears shifted so fast from verse to prose that I wondered what had happened. At first I thought it was the house. Then I thought it was the history of the previous owner. I considered Roland. Then it came to me clear and true. You were narrating just like you did as we drove around the places east of here. One day I went for a drive on my own. I found a little graveyard in the middle of a field. The gravestones had almost all Irish names. I found an Ennis O'Conner and his loving wife Siobahn. A story began to hatch in me head. You told me the rest of it."

"So what you're saying is I am your muse?"

"Yes, think of how we could inspire each other if we were together."

Well, I had to think about the 'together' part. Yeah, I definitely wanted to sit in the magic chair, but if he was suggesting I live up there with him…

"I guess we would be an amusing couple," I said, and instantly regretted the pun.

"Don't make fun of it."

"I don't know what to think."

"Sony…"

"No wait, I need to say all of this while it's clear in my head. I just found out today that you and Bim…Bim for God's sake, knew each other before you knew me. I then found out that you guys got together to ransom me from a guy that you grew up with. And then you tell me he is a spy and now he may have what, eliminated the guy who tried to kill me."

"You're still in shock."

"No, what I'm doing is trying to digest it, Desmond. All of this 'news' comes on top of the fact that your novel pleased and upset me at the same time. Do you understand what a freaking mess my brain is right now?"

"Let's make it simple. Do you love me?"

I looked at him with my mouth hanging open. Was he that dense?

"You just asked me the hardest question of all."

"And your answer?"

It was getting cold in the room. I thought I could hear the roof creaking above me and thought it might be the snow. It was coming down so hard right now that the yard light looked like a distant nebula. Des and I had come down to the main issue: love. Amidst all my own brain static came a moment of clarity. This voice, I noted was my own.

"The answer to that question is I don't know. I need some time to think. I know you bought this house so I assume you are going to live in it for a while. Well, I plan on living down below for a while, too. I think we should give it a rest, Des. I don't feel that kind of love for you right now. Is that honest enough for you?"

"I think I see."

"I hope so."

"Did you ever feel it?"

Men are idiots.

"I felt it immediately. And then it sort of faded. If it sounds weird I'm sorry."

The silence of the snow followed. There was no expression to read for either of us. I guess we both stared at faint silhouettes filled with emotion, but mute. I heard him clear his throat.

"It's snowing pretty hard out there. Do you want to spend the night on the couch?"

I hadn't really thought about my exit yet. I glanced at the window and saw nothing that would invite me out into the storm. I also could not visualize a tomorrow morning there.

"I'm going to walk home tonight, Des. It's all down hill from here."

CHAPTER THIRT-FIVE

MOLLY

Christmas. Like most long-awaited events this one has arrived. The weather is cold, but the sun is shining bright on the most recent layer of the many snows we have had so far this winter. As I look out the kitchen window here at Ghost Farm, I see a driveway full of cars. Besides the ones that belong here, there is the Pat Stouffer's old Buick that brought her and Bim over. Mike and Carrie came in Bim's classic Chevy, which they have been using during their extended visit. I see the rental Jeep that Mel and Ray have been driving and now, better late than never, and riding what looks to be Meg Bollander's old red ATV, is my neighbor, Des O'Conner.

I got most of the story from Sony about where she and he stand. I notice now that he is shy around her, while she pretends nothing is different. Poor man; he got his freedom from his ex-wife and ironically, my daughter won't give him the true prize of that freedom. And yet she still wears his Claddagh. Well, as Roland used to say, life is tricky. Des came in the back door as usual.

"Merry Christmas, Molly Costello. I hope I'm not late."

"Maybe a little, but we are about to eat so you are just in time. What are you riding there?" I said and nodded out the window.

"I found it in the barn up there. Still had the keys in it. I called the realtor and she said whatever was on the property was mine."

"Meg used to ride that thing all over the countryside."

"It's pretty good over the snow."

"So it seems."

Des seemed to be a bit skitterish around me still. It was the first time we had spoken to each other since the day Sony

189

and I went up there. I really wanted to let him off the hook, at least as far as I was concerned.

"Des, I am happy you decided to come down here today."

"Well, I had to think it over. You know…?"

"Yeah, I know. She's in the living room with the others."

He gave me a wan smile as he headed into the other room. It had to be awkward for him with Sony estranged and Mel still holding him in contempt. Through the open door I saw Sony look up and smile at him. A moment later when I followed him in, I saw Melanie get up and pull her fist back like she was going to punch him. Instead she melted into a smile and gave the poor man a hug. Apparently, the sisters had been talking.

I sat down on the couch next to my husband and listened to the banter.

"So the fookin' Irish have arrived," said Bim. He was feeling good about his eggnog.

"I have, Bim," said Des. "I love the little green Christmas vest. Makes you look like one of Santa's fookin' leprechauns"

"You got that right," said Pat. "Merry Christmas, Des."

Des found a chair and Mike handed him an eggnog. He took a quick sip and winced.

"Jaysus, Michael, what did you put in this?"

"Just a little Vitamin K, Des. Merry Christmas."

"Merry Christmas, Des," said Carrie, her icy blue eyes dancing like the angel atop the tree. "And congrats on the house. You going to stay in Wisconsin forever now?"

"Merry Christmas to you, too, Carrie. And yes, I'm planning on staying for a while."

"You ever want to do some remodeling up there, I think I still have some dynamite in the garage," Bim quipped. Des rolled his eyes.

Mike was taking pictures as usual and was framing Desmond. "Smile," Mike said. Des made a face.

"Nice one, Des," said Mike. "They told me at Stompe to get a jacket photo of you. Now you've done it!"

"Once a fool, always a fool," Des murmured, as if to no one. I knew better.

"I heard your book will be out this spring," said Owen.

Des acknowledged it: "I hear that, too."

"I can't wait to read it," said Pat. She was so proud of her short gray hair that had finally started to sprout back. She looked both healthy and stylish.

"You're going to love it," said Sonia and everyone sort of got quiet and deferred to her. "I would like to propose a toast." She held her eggnog high and everyone else did too, except for Des. "Here's to the best writer since Roland Heinz."

"Here, here," said everyone.

"Thank you, Sony," said Des, "though here I am sitting in his house with his family and me feet too small to fill the great man's shoes."

"Me feet too small," Bim mimicked. Everyone laughed as Des smiled and shook his head.

"Can't slip even a kind word past you, Bimster," Des said.

"Not when it's coated in Irish bullshit!" roared Bim.

I had to jump in. "Please everyone, come to the table."

Carrie, Mel, and Sony leapt up and hurried to the kitchen and started the process of carrying food to my dining table. We hardly ever used that space and it was fun to set a holiday table and fill it with the people I love.

After dinner we had coffee, pie, and opened presents. I was pleased that my Taos gifts were cherished. The Bollander oil that Owen had bought me had arrived and was already hung where a mirror used to hang in the living room. Although it was a painting of New Mexico, it looked at home facing Lake Winnebago, the place that first inspired its artist to pick up a brush.

I think I may have been the only one watching as Sonia and Desmond exchanged gifts. They did it apart from everyone else over by the window in the living room. They are really an astonishing couple when you see them together. I was hoping they wouldn't notice me watching them, but I guess I didn't need to worry about that. I saw him give her a small box and heard him say he'd brought it back from Ireland. When she opened it, I saw the soft glow of gold, but it was not a ring or any other piece of jewelry. It was a rather stylistic, old looking key, like it might be for the front door of a castle.

She then gave him a box which revealed a rusted antique lock, the sort used on barn doors around here a hundred years ago. They thanked each other with a smile and a nod that I knew probably said more than a kiss. Gee, a rusty lock and a gold key. I couldn't help but think that it was the beginning of another family mystery that only time would unravel. I turned away and felt lighter in my heart. Poets!

The mood was perfect as the sun began its swift drop onto that lake ice and shot an orange glow into the room. Our group was a little quieter now, subdued perhaps by the big meal and all the talking. Melanie was the last one out of the kitchen and as she came in and sat down, Pat broke the silence.

"You shouldn't be working so hard, Mel." She nodded at Mel's tummy.

"Oh, a little work keeps me fit."

"Well, you certainly are that. I was as big as a house with Carrie. She was a load."

"Oh Mom," Carrie moaned.

"Well, you were. Little Ray there looks like he'll be tiny."

I saw Mel glance at her husband and their eyes met.

"Well, actually, Ray and I have thought it over and we think there are enough Crazy Ray's in this world. Our son will be called Roland Heinz Hitowkski."

I am not ashamed to say, I cried immediately. I couldn't help it, All day long I had been thinking about Roland. He was everywhere in this house and in the lives of everyone that was here today. He was our Papa, our benefactor, our friend, our inspiration, our protector, our rainy day man, and our friendly ghost. Everything I saw was full of him. His ashes may have been out back by the lilac bushes with Sorry, his dog; but his spirit was as alive as Melanie and Ray's eminent child.

I often wondered what life would have been like if I had never taken that interview assignment years ago and come to Ghost Farm in the first place. What if Roland's dream had different characters? I would never have met Owen for one thing. With that thought I whispered in his ear.

"Let's go for a walk. I want to show you something. No need to bundle up. It's in the barn."

I led him outside and across the yard to the yellow barn. We passed through the animal clinic and into the cavern that held so many of Roland's things. I sat down in one of the three old lawn chairs that sat in the middle of this drafty cathedral in Pipe, Wisconsin. Owen eased in beside me. The only light in the barn was the last light of the day that came down from the glazed over holes in the roof high above us.

"Listen." I whispered.

A few seconds later we heard some scratching coming from up in the rafters. Then the beating of mighty wings.

"What's that, honey? Is there an owl up there again?"

"No listen."

Then it came. A 'caw' so loud that it echoed off the walls and floor. Then another 'caw' louder than the first.

"Crows?" asked Owen.

"Two of them. I noticed them about a week ago. They seem to have come to stay."

"How'd they get in?"

"Oh, there are still ways to get in here. Especially, if you're a bird."

"So we have crows now."

"Not just crows, honey, messenger birds."

"You'd better fill me in."

"Bim reminded me that Roland wrote about messenger birds. Birds that were sent to set up an arc in his stories. I checked it out and he used crows as messengers in all of his books. That includes the early ones about Viet Nam, too. The common thread was this device. Messenger birds."

"Crows."

"Exactly."

"And what exactly do these messenger birds in our barn have to say."

I leaned over and gave my love a kiss on his scarred cheek.

"Just listen..."

EPILOGUE

"What are they doing, Father?

"They are finishing a book, Garnet."

"Which book is that? I don't see a book They have nothing in their hands."

"Books are not always held in the hand, my dear. They are often held fast in the mind and in the heart. Think on it, girl. Some characters never take a breath of earthly air and yet they breathe the same essence of life that these barn-sitters do."

"And garage-sitters, too, right?"

"You do pick up things fast, don't you?"

"I don't know what I do, I just do it."

"Exactly! To live where we do requires nothing, but someone taking the time to think of us and write us down."

"And why then did that person turn us into birds and place us in this barn?"

"Because that is where we are supposed to be right now. This is what that person who writes is dreaming about at this moment."

"And them two below are what, dreams or dreamers?"

"They are both."

"I'm confused again, Father."

"Ah well, darlin', nothing in any form of existence is simple and no one who exists is who others think they are. Do this, girl, just say 'caw' every couple of minutes…and stay out of that bathtub!

And everywhere there were birds.

ACKNOWLEDGEMENTS

Roland Heinz would never have lived without the help of:

Paula J. Barton
Mark B. Miller
Fuller McBride
John McCarcins
Alicia McCareins
Cheryl Krebs
Tom Guilfoile
Jim Schroeder
Leah Tultle
W.L. Harris
And
Amy Zangl

231115LV00001B/26/P

9 781457 502491